Raven

by

Tim Pearsall

"across silent landings, up twisting stairways, along dusty corridors past empty bedrooms until she reached the cleansing silver and shadow of the moonlit upper floors"

Chapters

Raven

A decaying mansion house, England - 2000

She stares from the window while the house sleeps. Memories of gone-by times an agony of regret. A fox runs silently across the moonlit lawn, she turns away. The room is silent but for the distant ticking of the grandfather clock in the great hallway.

The fireplace holds warm embers, she catches a glimpse of herself in the mirror above, black hair and dark emerald eyes. She frowns as an ancient memory flashes monochrome through her mind:-

A churchyard in old Tudor England, a priest falls back, a bloody knife wound deep in his chest.
His voice, so deep,
"Curse you Witch!..." He coughs blood, "...And I name thee Raven!..." His final utterance, "...I Curse your treacherous black serpent heart!..." She wiped his blood from her blade as he fell,
"You can't curse me..." She saw death take him, "...I've been damned already."

She pushed the memory aside and returned to the window. The fox had gone.

Cairo

Egypt ~ 1985

Raven held her baby tightly and scowled at the people teeming on the street below. Cairo, her baby, suckled on her thumb. While Cairo the city, lay simmering before her. She turned to her baby,

"I'm so sorry..." She muttered to her wide-eyed infant, nodding down to the swarm of cars and people on the street below, "...Never trust them, not one of them. They will fail you. All of them..." She turned her emerald green eyes away from the thronging street to stare into the warm trusting eyes of her baby, "...For when you fall in fear and pain, they will not come to you."

She stepped back into the room, where the father of the baby lay unconscious. A soft but urgent knock turned her eyes to the door, she called out,

"Who's there?" It was Franco, he spoke through the closed door,

"The car is ready mistress." Seconds later she faced him in the doorway saying,

"He..." She motioned to the man prostrate on the floor, "...Will not be coming."

Chapter 1
"Your pain is my pleasure..."

A hotel room, London ~ 2000

A dark-haired beauty speaks, her voice suggestive of pleasures to come,

"Let me fix you another drink first," She pushes the man away with a smile, her sparkling green eyes full of promise, and pours the wine quickly, making sure the little pill in his glass has fully dissolved. She downs the rest of her champagne,

"Salut." Then lifts his glass to his lips, encouraging him to do the same.

Inside her mind, deep in that dark recess, she can feel his lust. It is fuel for a craving all of her own.

The wine bottle is left behind as she eases him backwards into the bedroom. While he gropes and paws, she deftly removes his clothing, lays him on his back, head on the pillow, naked and breathless with excitement. He stares at her in fascination, ignoring the strange numbness that has begun in his legs.

Strange, beguiling and sensuous, she strips away her own clothing and casts it away through the open bedroom door. Black silk underwear gives way to warm amber skin, soon she is naked but for an unusual soft leather garter. A sheath for a pale shimmering dagger.

"For protection." She purrs. He tries to reach for her, but the creeping numbness is now a total paralysis. In sudden fear he looks up into her face. She smiles, teeth white and perfect, green eyes as cold as death. With a sigh of anticipation she quickly ties back her hair with an

1

elastic band, unsheathes the brutal silver blade, and looms over him like a ravenous animal.

She hungers. He tries to speak, to shout in terror; but nothing will come. She straddles his legs,

"You can't move, but you **can** feel pain..." She raises the blade to his throat, "..And fear." Teasing the skin, before moving the point to his chest.

"This..." It slides between his ribs, "...Will..." She twists it, "...Hurt!"

It was the purest agony. His eyes bulge and water, his brain hammers. And how she loves it! From the instant of his suffering she swims in ecstasy, groaning and shuddering with an earthy physical delight.

The minutes pass, and as his suffering increases, so her ecstasy rises. She uses the knife more carelessly, each agony inflicted bringing her closer to a frenzied climax until she can prolong it no more. With a shout she plunges the dripping blade deep into his chest sending a fountain of blood into the air. The man sees through tear-filled eyes as she pushes her face into the ruby fountain of his blood and stares down at him. Her green eyes wide and unblinking, her body quivering like a plucked wire.

At the moment of his death she cries out and collapses on him, exhausted, squirming in his gory remains, gasping in the aftermath of orgasm.

Eventually she peels herself off him, wipes herself down with a bed sheet and enters the shower.

As always she leaves no evidence of her presence, and she exits the hotel room unseen.

Outside in the street it is dark and raining, a shiny black car glitters wet in the lamplight, for a moment the street is filled with the sound of Barbieri's Don Quixote as she opens the rear door, moments later they are gone.

London, Windsor - 2000

The following February morning arrived bright and cold. Richard Bryant walked to work, hands in his pockets, collar turned up. A young man, he was a partner in a small printing business founded five years earlier with a school friend. Their premises were in the quaint old part of Windsor, little more than a mile from where Richard and his pale blue-eyed wife Susan had a mortgage on a small modern townhouse.

He enjoyed the exercise, often changing his route in order to investigate some of the old hidden alleyways and historic buildings. One of his favourites was a large three storey Victorian town house, the lower part of which had long since been converted into a second-hand bookshop. , The Windsor Scientific brimmed with pamphlets; travel guides, maps, science journals, magazines and comics, as well as a vast number of well-thumbed paperbacks. Above the peeling doors there was a faded quotation in gold paint:

'A prudent man does not make the goat his gardener'

The shopkeeper was a man who appeared as old and ruined as many of his books, Dr Von Vohberg. Each morning he would haul out the patched old canvas canopy before dragging out his trestle tables topped with bargain or 'one for the way home' books. Richard would say good morning as he passed by; the withered old man would turn slowly, smile and return his greeting in a grave and deeply accented voice. Richard was surprised then, when he turned the corner to find the canopy still up and the shop closed. As he neared he saw the doors swing open and the back of a tall slim man come shuffling backwards, dragging a trestle.

3

"Good morning." Richard announced out of habit, The man turned slowly, much in the manner of the old man, and nodded.

"My father is ill..." His voice was deep, grave, and with an east European accent, "...A message would you like me to accept for him?" Richard was caught out; he hadn't expected a conversation. The tall son continued,

"I am Walther, of his two sons the youngest. I am looking after the shop until he is well again." He held out his hand. Richard felt a little awkward, realising that Walther had mistaken him for a friend of his father.

"Sorry to hear that, I hope he's on his feet again soon..." Shaking the tall man's hand as he spoke, "...Actually I don't really know him that well." He confessed under the man's penetrating gaze.

"Ah. I see." There was a moment of awkward silence before Richard carried on his way.

A little farther on he bought a morning newspaper, The headline ran,

The New Ripper: Another Victim!

The tabloids had been busy inventing increasingly bizarre theories about the identity and motives of the new London serial killer.. Richard had already flipped the paper around to the sports section by the time he reached the short driveway leading up to his premises.

He was pleased to see his business partner's car parked neatly in its usual spot, Phil was always in early. Philip Leach had been Richard's friend in high school, his best man when he'd married Susan, and as friends and equal partners they had started up in business.

A roadside campfire, England ~ 2000

On a dark, cold night a smoking campfire lit the man's face, his stubbled Asian features belied a deep and cultured voice,

"We are born with envy, we are consumed by it..." The man muttered through the smoke of his camp fire, staring, not at his companion, a drunken hag sprawled semi-conscious in a deck chair facing him, but into the flames and at the world that lay beyond their glowing circle, "...It makes dogs of men. turns friend against friend..." The firelight glowed hot in his eyes, "...Turns lovers into~" Smoke drifted across his face, stinging his unflinching eyes. In time he closed them, letting his mind roam high on to the astral plane, searching, always searching, hoping for another glimpse of her.

*

A house in the Countryside ~ 2000

Her long black hair streaming behind, teenage Cairo dashed along the forgotten and dusty twilit secret corridors of the rambling old mansion house.

Whilst playing a frantic game of 'It' with her imaginary friends she'd lost her bearings and popped through a tiny wooden door hidden beside a long-abandoned welsh dresser. Stopped dead in her tracks, staring, her eyes unnaturally wide from the gloom, she realised with a sick feeling where she was. The cellar.

"This place gives me the horrors!" She whispered to her friends as she wiped sweat from her pale almond face with the back of her hand. Rooted to the spot, she stared at the heavily bolted wooden door that led to Sir Clive's laboratory, her voice was a quiet hiss,

"And **he** gives me the **double** horrors!" She turned her gaze away from the door and parted the cobwebbed hair hanging limp across her face. Without turning her head, her eyes roved the walls and ceiling. The windowless corridor was dirty with years of neglect, the light sick and yellow from a single weak bulb. With a sudden shiver she imagined a million vile insects crawling through the soft plaster and sagging timbers. Then, with another, deeper shudder, she remembered the last time she'd found herself down there in the cellar. Involuntarily, she turned to face the dresser, where she had crouched, hidden inside the 'dog-kennel' and watched in fear as Sir Clive led a young woman into his laboratory, a red glow on their faces from the open doorway.

"And there were others." She wiped her sticky palms vigorously against the side of her ragged white cotton dress, and then turned again quickly, startled at the sound of approaching footsteps.

"It's him!..." She warned her friends. Remembering something she had overheard in the kitchen, her voice now a breathless whisper, "...He's as mad as a hat-stand you know!"

Like a startled cat she leapt back through the tiny opening beside the dresser into the sanctuary of her catacombs, scampering swiftly and silently upwards through the secret innards of the house. Across silent landings, up twisting stairways, along dusty corridors past empty bedrooms until she reached the cleansing silver and shadow of the moonlit upper floors.

London, Windsor ~ 2000

Richard strode cheerfully up the steps to Reception, "Morning Cyndy..." He called over his shoulder while hanging his jacket. "...Out last night?"

"Yeah..." Her reply came through pursed lips as she applied her lipstick, "...I dumped Mike last night." She remarked, deadpan, while turning her attention to sorting the morning's mail. Richard laughed; he had long ago given up trying to keep track of Cyndy's boyfriends. She was short and pretty, hair in a messy blonde bob, although that changed almost as often as her boyfriends. She gave the false impression of being the archetype blonde bimbo, often turning the tables on an unsuspecting 'male sexist arsehole'.

The busy morning passed by as quickly as usual and it was soon lunchtime. Richard and Phil often took lunch together in a nearby pub, the Seven Stars, nothing fancy, just a pint and a sandwich, but they enjoyed the break from work and the chance to chat like friends. Since Richard had married they had stopped meeting in the evenings as often as they used to, not because Susan had been awkward about it, things had just changed. The pub was already busy when they arrived at just after one o'clock and they were lucky to find two stools by the window.

Halfway through his sandwich Richard mentioned the bookshop,

"It'll be a shame if the old place closes down." Phil shrugged,

"Everything changes eventually, and it is a bit of an eyesore." Richard put down his sandwich in mild annoyance,

7

"No, no it's not an eyesore. It's got character, unlike most of the new bland, corporate-image designer-bollocks shop fronts going up in the high street today." He waved a dismissive hand indicating the fashion shops and burger bars that lined the busy shopping street.

"Every street in every town looks the same, same shops, same products, Same bland faces." There was a slight pause before Philip restarted the conversation,

"So, do you know the old boy who owns it then?" Richard finished chewing before answering.

"No. Not really, but funnily enough I met his son this morning. He assumed I knew his dad, I don't know why but I've got the strangest feeling about it." Phil gave him a sideways look,

"So, is this another one of your famous hunches?" Richard paused in thought for a moment, unable to explain his feelings,

"Oh I don't know, forget it, it's probably nothing."

"Hmm, we'll see." Phil had always admired Richard's intuitive grasp of things, how he could always see the whole of the moon when others just stared.

They sat in comfortable silence for a while, both gazing out of the window as the sky darkened and a light drizzle began to fall.

"We had better run for it."

Walther Von Vohberg, Windsor

At an antique wooden desk at the rear of the bookshop, Walther pored over his father's files and diaries, trying to get them into some sort of chronological order, *"The older ones are fine, but these..."* He shook his head at the pile of densely scribbled notebooks, *"...Ramblings."* He

8

opened one at random, reading the words quietly aloud,

"She will transfix her prey, secure under her gaze they will offer no resistance.

AT ALL COSTS AVOID THOSE EYES!"

He put the notebook down with a sigh of sadness.

Raven, a cage fight~ London

Raven didn't fight for the money. Her benefactor, Sir Clive, whom she had been blackmailing for years, made sure she wanted for nothing.

Raven didn't fight for the money, she fought for the sheer visceral pleasure of it. The problem was she was too good at it. She had quickly become a star, people followed her and that was bad. So she lost a few important fights and dropped from the limelight. After that she limited the frequency of her fights and made sure to lose a few for good measure.

Tonight she was up against Sparkle, a sassy, much touted young fighter who was tipped for stardom. Raven had already made up her mind to lose the fight without much pain, but that was until she got into the cage and Sparkle opened her mouth, taunting and mocking, grinning and threatening,

"Gonna smack~you~up, bitch!" Sparkle was tough, a semi~professional and a good boxer. Raven abandoned her plan to throw the fight and laid into her, *I'm going to knock that stupid grin off her face!*" She led with a kick, followed by quick jabs, Sparkle parried and jabbed back, quick on her feet, *"She's good."* Raven feigned a lunge, then swung into a kick across her legs. Sparkle went down but quickly rolled and hit Raven with a surprise high kick to the nose. The crowd roared at the sudden flow of blood, Sparkle bathed in the applause, and it was the half-second Raven needed to finish the fight. She poked Sparkle in the eye, grabbed her head and slammed her knee into her face, kicked her legs away and punched her to the floor. Sparkle was out.

London, Windsor

"We'd better run for it." Richard and Philip left the pub and returned to the office to be confronted by a stern faced Cyndy,

"You have a 'client' waiting in your office..." She uttered the word client like an oath. The two men looked surprised, knowing there were no appointments booked, "...She's been here fifteen minutes and if-" Richard interrupted her,

"Cyn, what is it? What's wrong?" She looked genuinely upset for a moment, then shrugged and put her face straight,

"I don't know, there's something about her, something weird. I don't like her, but it's more th-" She didn't have time to finish, all three of them turned at the sound of a woman's voice, a voice sweet and low, her diction impeccable but with a trace of a European accent,

"Do you expect me to wait for much longer?" The beautiful Raven-haired woman smiled delightfully as she finished her sentence, leaned against the door frame and tilted her head. Philip was the first to recover his composure; smiling from ear to ear he apologised for keeping her waiting and escorted her into his office, calling over his shoulder for Cyndy to provide coffees. She and Richard exchanged looks for a moment before she stomped off to the kitchen, muttering,

10

"Now where did I put that rat poison?" He smiled as she clattered around in the little kitchen.

A few minutes later Richard intercepted Cyndy in the corridor with the coffee tray,

"It's okay Cyn, I'll take them in for you."

Philip's office door was closed; Richard struggled for a second with the handle, and then strolled in wearing his most charming grin. Philip was sat at the side of his desk with the mysterious woman at its front; both were leaning forward and smiling. Richard felt more than a little unwanted, *"Three's a crowd"* He thought to himself as he set down the tray.

"Thanks Rich..." Philip sounded just a little sheepish, "...Listen; we can fit in a small rush order this week can't we?" They both knew the schedule was already full for the rest of the week at least, but Phil had given him a look; he wanted a favour. Richard was not going to let him off quite so easily,

"What sort of rush order?" He demanded bluntly. The workshop was printing flat out and a disruption could be costly.

"Oh it's just a few copies of some rare old books, you know, family heirlooms, that kind of thing."

"So why the 'rush'?" Richard teased him, kept him dangling for a few moments, and was very tempted to keep him there, but they had been friends for so long, and besides Phil had never had much luck with girls, so if it would help,

"Yes sure Phil, of course we can, no problem, book it in for the end of the week. I'll leave it for you to sort out." With a wink he turned and left the office, saying,

"Nice to meet you." To the woman as she fixed him with a green-eyed gaze.

11

A little while later Richard was in the print shop checking over the production schedules for later in the week when Cyndy strolled up and gave him a slip of paper. It was a note from Phil:

Rich, I'm taking the rest of the afternoon off, I'm going to pick up those books myself, it might speed things up, see you tomorrow, Phil.'

Richard and Cyndy just looked at each other and laughed,
"The dirty git, you wait til I see him tomorrow!"

A roadside campfire, England

In a litter-strewn lay-by at the side of the A34 south from Stratford-upon-Avon, the rugged Asian man once more stirred soup over an open fire. His companion, her face set in an unfriendly crumpled scowl, sipped from a flask and occasionally spat on the ground between her feet,
"Ain't that crap ready yet?" She gasped, barely able to speak, pointing at his soup, coughing and spitting again. The man, apparently unmoved by her rudeness, his voice smooth and resonant, had a habit of quoting from Shakespeare,
"When I was at home I was in a better place; but travelers must be content." He continued to gently stir his pot, his thoughts in the past, while the coarse calls of the crows from the nearby trees prompted him to whisper,
"He that doth the ravens feed, yea, providently caters for the sparrow."

London, Windsor

At home that evening Richard chatted with Susan, about the days events. She laughed when he told her about Phil's antics and promised to tease him about it when she next saw him. They had a good relationship; caring without being over-possessive and they enjoyed each others company. She worked in a department store and either of them could be first to get home. They ate mainly out of the freezer during the week and they both liked to get things ready for the others arrival, that usually entailed opening a bottle of wine, preparing some bread and salad, and putting something in the microwave. Tonight they'd had lasagne and leaves with some garlic bread, their evening had been comfortable and relaxing and as usual they went to bed together and had soon fallen asleep.

Richard had never suffered from nightmares:

He woke suddenly with that terrifying sense that someone else was in the room. Although it was dark he could still see clearly, everything seemed normal. Until he heard the breathing, like the panting of an animal, coming from below the edge of the bed on Susan's side. Very slowly he reached across and gently shook Susan, she didn't stir, he shook her again more firmly, again she didn't stir and then his hand felt warm and wet. He sat bolt upright, trembling. Susan lay naked beside him, dead, a long handled dagger embedded in her chest. From below the edge of the bed a face rose up, a girl child, a feral child with the eyes of an animal, she was on her knees. Blood dripped from her chin, the tiny gaps between her teeth stained red. She licked her lips and laughed, head back, almost a howl. Fixing Richard with eyes that have seen hell, she rose up, naked, and scampered around the bed to the door,

"Come with me." Her voice hummed like a swarm of insects. He leapt up and ran, through the bedroom door-

-into a hot red gravel wasteland. It wasn't day, and it wasn't night. The moon was high and shimmered a pale purple, the sun lay burnt orange on the horizon. He ran on, a hot dark path burned his bare feet, he too was naked. On either side of the path stood strangers cheering, urging him on. He had a knife in his hand.

He arrived at a house, alone in the wilderness; a palace made of sand and smoke. Through a doorway of fire and across a hallway of ice he came to a wide staircase of sandstone blocks. She waited at the top. On her hands and knees she grinned salaciously at him.

He mounted the steps, leaving imprints in the sandy blocks like footsteps on the shore. As he neared her she rolled over and bounced up on to her feet, urging him forward with her finger until they reached a bedroom.

The bed was a wide altar of ashes; she threw herself down backward sending up plumes of charcoal dust. She urged him on. Richard stood at the foot of the bed, knife in hand, ready to take her and then kill her. It was what she wanted. He knew it! He placed a knee on the bed and leaned forward.

And then he woke, shaking, shocked, confused and afraid. Susan was on her knees beside him; the bedside lamp was on.

"I couldn't wake you!..." She almost yelled, sounding concerned, "...Are you okay? I've been shaking you for ages." He pulled himself up into a sitting position, wet all over with sweat.

"God you're soaked!" She'd leaned forward and

14

touched his cheek.

"I'm okay, I need the bathroom..." He climbed off his sweat-damp side of the bed and trudged to the bathroom, "...Grab me a clean Tee shirt would you?" She took one from his drawer and followed him,

"Must've been some nightmare, what was it about?" She asked, watching him splash cold water on his face. Richard glared at his reflection in the mirror and asked himself, *"Good question - what the hell was it about?"* The dream had left him with a feeling of confusion and shame,

"I don't know, but it was so real, I've never dreamt so vividly before, it was like I was really there."

"Where?"

"I don't know, it was crazy, I thought I'd left..." He struggled for words, "...Gone into a different dimension or something."

"Like the Astral plane?"

"What?"

"Oh it's a like a parallel world or something."

"Yeah well it was weird enough."

"What happened?" He didn't want to tell Susan about the girl,

"It's gone already, I can't remember..." He lied, "...I was being chased by something."

The house in the Countryside - 2000

Cairo woke suddenly, aware of the scurrying feet of a mouse close by,

"Hello Mr Mouse." She lay underneath her bed with her teddy and other favourite things. Items mostly collected on her solitary wanderings of the vast old house. The hoard lay on a folded blanket and included a cigarette

15

lighter, toreador trinket box, straw hat and a crystal paperweight.

The house was very quiet, she could hear the ticking of the clock on the landing and knew that it must be around 02:00am.

The mouse had made her think of cheese, she rolled from under her bed in her slightly grubby pyjamas and set off for the kitchen. But not via the main staircase, as usual Cairo took to the darker passages. A few moments later she entered the kitchen via the servant's stairs, grabbed a plate and headed for the fridge. There was some cold meat, lots of cheese, and even a slice of pie. She took a swig of orange juice straight from the bottle, then stacked her plate,

"I hope Mr Mouse likes smelly cheese." She whispered in the ghostly hush of the rambling old house. And then in moments she had disappeared back into the dark passages,

"Coming Mr Mouse, I hope you're hungry."

Back in her bedroom she placed tea-lights on the floor and laid out a trail of tiny cheese crumbs for the mouse to follow. She fell asleep again just before dawn, happy to have played with her new friend, Mr Mouse.

Richard, Windsor

Richard rose late the next morning, Susan had already left for work, her commute was further and she always left first, but for some reason he missed her more that morning. He felt tired and nervy, the dream had upset him deeply, because of its contents, his apparent lust for the little girl and the murder of his wife had shaken him to the core., *"I'm no paedo, what the hell, it was so damn fucking real."*

His walk to work was tense, he felt distracted and wary, as if he was being watched. He hardly noticed where he was and was surprised when he was spoken to by the tall man outside the Windsor Scientific bookshop,

"Father is feeling a little better today, good morning." Richard stopped, looked up at the man, taking in his appearance, his academic-looking suit and thin moustache, a noble face.

"Oh that's good, must be a great relief for you." He managed to reply. And again felt hot under the tall man's gaze.

"I must see to the canopy. Good day." Richard felt like he'd been let off the hook and hurried on his way. He bought a newspaper as usual and cheered up a little at the sight of Phil's car parked in its usual place. He found himself eager to find out how he'd got on with the glamorous new client. In the reception Cyndy was sipping coffee and pointed with her pencil to the door of the print room,

"He's in there..." She obviously meant Phil, "...With a pile of knackered old books." Richard smiled, hung his jacket and went in to see him, his newspaper under his arm.

"Hi Phil. So, how did you get on with Madame Voluptua?" He joked and expected Phil to respond in a similar vein, he was disappointed,

"Hmm? Sorry Rich, what did you say? Sorry mate, I'm a bit busy at the moment." Phil hadn't even looked up. Richard stood there, apparently unnoticed for several more seconds before he tried again,

"So how many books are there? And how much rescheduling is there?" Phil was still too engrossed in his work to notice him.

"Philip!" He sharp tone had little effect,

17

"Umm? Listen Rich, why don't you just let me get on with this, 'the sooner the better' and all that?"

The effects of the nightmare and that vague feeling of unease all built up at once, Richard lost his cool, he grabbed Phil by the shoulders and spun him around so that they were face to face,

"Since when did you start running this business on your own? We're supposed to be partners, remember? You made me look like a fucking idiot in front of that woman yesterday and now you've completely wrecked our schedules just because you fancy the glossy tart!" Richard saw the expression on Phil's face change from surprise and indignation to an awful realisation. He slumped down heavily onto one of the nearby swivel chairs, a distant look on his face,

"Rich I'm sorry, I don't feel well." He shook his head as if to clear it and rubbed his temples. Richard was just about to apologise for ranting at him when Cyndy's voice made them both turn.

"Coffee time!..." She marched in with two steaming mugs, "...There's a complaint from the workforce, you know, the ones that do all the real work around here. They want to know how they're supposed to get anything done with all that shouting going on?" The two men sipped their coffees in brooding silence. Phil's weird behaviour further increasing Richard's disquiet. In the end Richard grudgingly apologised and agreed to leave Phil to get on with it. And then without knowing why, while Phil had turned away, he took the opportunity to pick up one of the smaller books and hide it inside his newspaper,

"See you for lunch?" Once again he received no reply.

London, Central

Raven was drawn down into the London Underground once more. Entering at Hammersmith she bought a day-ticket and made the half-hour trip on to Liverpool Street station where she changed to the Central Line. Far busier, where the passengers were at their most dense, she stood close to a couple whose body language gave away their recent arguments. Their mixed feelings of anger and fear hit her like the first cigarette of the day. Shortly she moved on. Boarding a train heading towards Oxford Circus, where, in times before CCTV, she could have wandered for hours if she'd wanted.

Impossible to completely hide her striking beauty, she dressed down, applied no make up (although she rarely did anyway) and pulled back her hair with a rubber band. She wanted anonymity, to feel without being noticed, to wallow in the waves of human emotion.

She spurned the opportunity of an empty seat, preferring to stand amongst the close packed commuters. After a time, she had no idea how long, she found herself next to a woman dressed in heels and a suit. Her eyes were hidden behind sunglasses but Raven knew they were puffy from crying. She followed her from the train, like a parasite greedily lapping at the slurry of emotion emanating from the unhappy woman.

It came to an abrupt end when the woman used a swipe card to enter a glass tower block, but already Raven had known the woman was close to her destination, the woman's mind had hardened, blocking off whatever it was that was upsetting her so much, steeling herself for another long day at a job she hated.

Raven blanked the change in emotion, like a cat

losing its prey, and returned to the Underground.

The house in the Countryside - 2000

Down in the cellar of a large old English mansion-house, Sir Clive, once a high ranking official of the British Foreign Office, polished his bright stainless steel surgical instruments and dreamed of immortality.

He didn't notice his multiple nightmarish reflections in the mirror-like bowls, scalpels, saws and tweezers, his bright bald head and mad, obsessive beady eyes.

"It's in the brain..." He repeatedly muttered to himself. "...They nearly had it, those great Victorian men of science, they nearly had it!..." He dropped his tools as a thought crossed his mind, "...Here." He tapped a forefinger on the side of a lifelike plastic human head. The lines at the corners of his eyes tightening as he grinned with a certain knowledge,

"I believe I have it!..." A maniacal grin, "...In the hypothalamus!"

London, Windsor

Richard closed his office door, a thing he rarely did, and sat behind his desk with the little old book held before him just below the desk's edge. Dark red in colour, the cover thick leather with the title long ago worn off, it seemed such an innocent little thing, *"Might be a family bible..."* Very carefully turned back the thick cover and opened it at the first page. In the background, he could hear Cyndy answering the phone, everything seemed quite ordinary, *"...So why am I shaking?"* The book contained text in Latin; he couldn't read a word of it. There were however, a great many sketches, drawings, and diagrams. It was divided into sections; the first part contained drawings of various tools and implements that he could not discern the use of. The second part depicted many naked men and women with detailed notes beneath them and arrows pointing to different parts of their bodies. It occurred to Richard that it might be a primitive medical journal of some kind and he kept on carefully turning the dry old pages.

The third section showed the same naked bodies except that this time they were accompanied by the tools from section one. The bodies were mutilated, torn and broken by the disembodied hands holding the now vicious looking implements. He realised with a sick feeling in his stomach that it was no medical journal, but an instruction manual for the systematic torture of human beings. He pressed on into section four, noting that there was a name and town at the top of each page, beneath the name was a picture of either a man or woman being mutilated by the implements. At the bottom of each of those pages was a single line of text, the same text repeated over and over again. He thought it might be in Latin but wasn't sure. From out of nowhere Cyndy's voice made him jump,

"Is that one of her ladyship's books?..." She stood in front of his desk, "...Must be very interesting, you didn't even notice me come in. Can I go to lunch now?" With a start, Richard saw that it was twelve o'clock; he had been poring over the book for more than an hour. His mind raced,

"Cyn, do you mind taking a later lunch today? There's someone I need to see. I'll be back by one!" He almost ran out of the office without another word. Cyndy

21

glared after him and then slammed back into her chair,

"They've flipped! Both of them." She moaned to herself as she picked up the phone to call a friend.

Richard found himself out in the street, in the cold without a jacket. He'd left the office in a kind of daze, the contents of the little book appalled him, and somehow he knew that the mysterious woman's other books were going to be the same, or worse. His thoughts turned to Philip, *"What the hell's he getting into?"* He had all questions and no answers, *"Who said there's no such thing as coincidence?"* He asked himself, standing outside the bookshop. Peering through the gloom he spied Walther sitting at a desk in the far corner, head down as if reading. He entered, pleased to find the shop empty, taking the book out of his pocket as he approached. Walther looked up and smiled politely. He seemed about to speak but Richard cut in first,

"I would like your opinion of this." His abruptness caused no more than a slightly raised eyebrow as Walther accepted the book from him. He studied its cover for a few moments and took out a magnifying glass from his desk drawer, then with an air of sudden interest, opened it seemingly at random. The seconds ticked by on the old shop clock and Richard started to feel a little foolish. He asked himself, *"Why am I doing this? It's only a book."* Walther's face had changed from an expression of polite interest to one of barely concealed agitation.

"From whom did you receive this atrocity?" He slammed the book shut, his tone demanding an explanation. The shop was still empty, the noise from the street faint and distant, drowned out by the ticking clock. Walther continued to demand an explanation,

"Such a book can not be yours. I ask you again, how is

22

it in your possession?" Richard had never been one to be bullied,

"Hold on. I brought the book to you, remember? You're supposed to be answering my questions!" Walther rose from behind the desk, a full six inches taller than Richard, with an air of quiet dignity he crossed to the door and locked it shut.

"What the hell are you doing?" Richard raised his voice warily. Walther held up a placating hand,

"Please. Come with me..." He led Richard through a faded curtain to a small cluttered room at the back of the shop, "...Sit, please..." And motioned to a worn leather armchair, "...I will tell you all I can about the book. And in return, you will tell me where its owner is to be found."

"Yes, er, I mean no, I can't..." Richard babbled, "...I have to get the book back before he notices it's missing."

"I see. Then perhaps we should meet later, after you finish work perhaps?"

"I can't just give you someone's address, that's a breach of-"

"Do you know what it's made of?"

"What? What's that got to do with- "

"The cover..." Walther handed the book back to Richard, "...Is made of human skin."

The house in the Countryside - 2000

Cairo sat cross-legged beneath her bedroom window. For perhaps the thousandth time in her life, she brushed her shining black hair aside and carefully turned the faded pages of an old magazine, 'Film Review and the Stars 1961-62'. As usual she stopped and stared at the portrait of Marlon Brando, carefully tracing the contours of

23

his face with her forefinger.

"Isn't he handsome?" She whispered. Her friends silently agreed.

Eventually she slid the magazine under her bed, rose and gazed out of the securely locked window.

London, Windsor

Richard had returned to the office in a state of distraction, he had agreed to meet Walther after work and trade with him the address of the mysterious woman for information about her. He looked after reception while Cyndy had lunch, grateful that the phone didn't ring too often, and managed to slip the book back with the others while Philip wasn't looking. It had been irritatingly easy; Philip hadn't even turned around to acknowledge his return from lunch. *"It's all in my mind."* He told himself, *"There's nothing sinister going on."* But he couldn't shake off the nagging unease. Taking up a sheet of paper, he decided to try his usual problem solving technique of writing things down. In large pink highlighter he wrote the titles to three columns; Woman with books, Philip, and Dream. It didn't help.

The afternoon dragged fretfully by until it was home time. Cyndy left on the stroke of five, Richard followed shortly afterwards, leaving Philip to lock up alone. The early evening was dark and cold; moisture hung in the air and settled on the glistening wet parked cars. The bookshop was already closed and in darkness. As he approached he saw a tall silhouette waiting in the doorway, Walther stepped out of the gloom.

"We have a bargain my friend..." His tone was expectant, and he placed himself directly in Richard's

24

path, "…You have the address, yes?" Richard stopped abruptly, annoyed at his tone but still eager to talk to him,

"Yes, I've got it. But before I give it to you I want a lot more information, I want to know why you want it so badly." Walther hesitated for just a second,

"Very well, but perhaps we should go somewhere more comfortable?" Richard agreed and led him to his usual pub, half full with people on their way home from work. They found seats by the imitation real fire, Richard with a pint of beer and Walther with a large glass of red wine.

"Forgive me if I ramble a little. There is much to tell. Perhaps too much…" Walther explained, "…You may have read in the scientific journals recently of the discovery of a new part of the brain? Yes? No? Well the theory is that they can now control the part of the brain that causes the ageing process. To such a point that it may be possible to halt it altogether. Eternal life may be just around the corner." He paused as Richard interrupted,

"What's that got to do with-"

"Please? Let me finish before you bombard me with questions." They both took sips from their drinks before he resumed,

"In my country it has been known for centuries that some people have extraordinarily long lives. These people are mutations, the part of the brain that has now become known to science does not function in the normal way and they live 'forever'. It is well known that the brain sends out signals to the body using electronic pulses, what is not so well known is that these pulses are also broadcast out into the air, as brain 'waves' if you like. The mutants that I am speaking about are able to receive these brainwaves, and it is the act of receiving them that stalls the gland that

25

governs the ageing process. And so the net result is that the person does not get older..." His next sentence was delivered in a flat monotone, "...These mutants have been known in my country for many centuries as the undead." Richard nearly choked on his beer,

"Oh for Christ's sake! You're telling me you're a fucking vampire hunter?" Walther continued his tale, quite unruffled,

"Scientists have been studying the power and intensity of brainwaves for many years and have reached the not surprising discovery that when a person is suffering some kind of stress or trauma their brain wave emissions increase dramatically. With physical pain causing the greatest increase in brainwave activity. The undead that I speak of are not blood-sucking vampires, my friend, they feed on the brain 'waves' of others. And I'm sure you can see that people who are suffering make a much more satisfying 'meal' than those who are not. Do you follow?" Richard nodded, speechless again.

"So, these Undead become gradually addicted to the intensity of suffering people, dependent on them as drug-users are to their habit." He paused for a while, allowing Richard time to digest his story and ask a question,

"How do you know all this? How come it hasn't been all over the newspapers?" Walther replied indirectly,

"My father studied these creatures for most of his life, after he met one when he worked in a Nazi concentration camp. She went by the name Raven Navaja and was not a prisoner; she was the mistress of the Commandant, an officer in Hitler's Schutzstaffel, or SS as they are better known. My father was conscripted to help with the disposal of the prisoners; he escaped eventually

26

and joined the Resistance movement. He was a good man, god rest his soul." Walther fell quiet and Richard realised with a shock that his father, the man who ran the bookshop, must have died, he could think of nothing to say and after a time Walther continued,

"I found him this afternoon, half out of bed. The doctor assured me that there would have been little or no suffering. I do not wholly believe him. His heart stopped. We already own a private plot in the cemetery, I will arrange a burial as soon as possible." He fell silent again; his eyes sparkling with unshed tears. Richard fetched more drinks giving him the time to compose himself. On Richard's return Walther was himself again and began talking immediately, the flickering fire lending a reddish glow to his face,

"Perhaps I should get to the point at last. A few weeks ago my father wrote to me where I was working in Vienna, he said that he had at last tracked down the creature he'd met at the concentration camp all those years ago. She was here in London and was responsible for the recent spate of, erm, rather gory murders. He went on to say that his health was deteriorating rapidly and that I was needed. Since my arrival two weeks ago I have read his many copious notes and listened to his advice. I am ready to complete his mission and destroy the monster. The main problem would have been finding her, but now, by an extraordinary coincidence, she has come to me. I believe the owner of that little book is the creature I seek." Richard pursed his lips, a sceptical look on his face.

"Just let me get this straight. You want me to give you the address of a woman you've never seen so that you can go and kill her? Is that right? Doesn't that make me an accomplice to murder?" There was no mistaking the sarcasm in his tone. Once again Walther was unflustered,

"Strictly speaking Richard, yes. Except that this creature is not on any census forms, has no nationality and possibly is not even wholly 'human'. I prefer to think of the killing as a service to mankind, she or it, should not be allowed to live." It was too much for Richard,

"No way, I'm out of here, you're insane!" He rose hurriedly to leave, Walther rose after him and called out at his departing figure,

"We have a bargain, remember. Think it over. Come to the shop tomorrow."

*

Richard hurried home along the black wet streets, haunted by the vision that Philip was in danger. Once indoors, he quickly opened a bottle of wine and poured himself a large glassful, aware that Susan would home very soon. He was draining his glass when she arrived, he hurried to meet her in the hallway and helped her off with her coat, realising in the back of his mind that he was a bit drunk. She sniffed his breath,

"You've been to the pub!" He coaxed her into the kitchen, sat her down and presented her with a glass of wine and the biscuit jar.

"We need to talk." He announced after clumsily slamming the fridge door and dropping the block of cheese.

"You see there's this woman..."

After a very bad start he eventually managed to tell Susan the whole story. The wine bottle was empty by the time the tale was finished and Susan's many questions answered. She'd become thoughtful,

28

"I'm worried about Phil. Do you think he really could be in danger? Shouldn't we warn him?" They decided to sleep on it.

Richard awoke at seven the next morning with a hangover. He left Susan in bed while he fortified himself with coffee and paracetamol before staggering off to work. The cold morning sunlight hurt his eyes but the walk refreshed him a little. Passing the bookshop he saw a hand written sign taped to the glass door,

"Closed owing to bereavement" With a cold shudder he hurried on around the corner and saw Phil stepping out of his car.

"Hey Phil!" He was delighted to see him, they went into the office together and Phil switched on the coffee machine,

"You look a bit worse for wear this morning..." Phil commented dryly, "...Did you and Sue go out last night?" Richard was careful with his reply,

"It's a bit of a long story, and I'll tell you later. Oh, by the way, Cyndy needs the address of your client so that she can send the invoice." He had tried to sound nonchalant with the request but could tell immediately that Phil had gone on the defensive,

"No need. She's paying cash and values her privacy." Richard couldn't believe it,

"What about the VAT?" Phil was dismissive,

"Oh don't worry, I'll sort it out, I'll lose it somewhere." It was obvious that Phil wasn't going to give out her address and he ended their brief conversation abruptly before going to the printing room. Richard waited alone in reception, staring at Phil's jacket hanging neatly in its usual place. For the first time in is life he went through

29

someone else's pockets, inside Phil's wallet he found an address on a slip of paper, 22 Old Bridge Lane, Hammersmith,

"Hi Richard!" Cyndy clattered in dropping her handbag and umbrella on the desk and immediately turning towards the mirror.

"Morning Cyn." He muttered as cheerfully as he could manage while he dropped Phil's wallet back inside his jacket unnoticed.

Raven, London

Raven's bouts of self-loathing came and went. Whatever chemicals stirred her brain to such atrocious acts of violence also kept her mood balanced. But occasionally she fell off-balance, and became suicidally depressed, *"It's all pointless, everything..."* She wandered the streets of central London, *"...And everybody."* Eventually sitting in one of the little garden squares between the bustling streets. She sat, cold, facing down, alone, until dusk.

A pair of black work-boots stopped in front of her, a voice,

"You alright love?..." The voice continued, "...Only I'm locking up soon, right?..." A rattle of keys, "...The gardens is closed for the night..." Another rattle, "...Can you hear me? Are you alright?"

Raven rose without a word and walked stiffly from the garden, the caretaker nodded, and muttered under his breath,

"Bleeding nutter."

Richard & Susan

Susan phoned Richard at the office to say that she was coming in to see him, she had been brooding over last nights revelations and decided that they had best talk to Walther as soon as possible. She arrived late morning; Richard heard her chatting briefly with Cyndy before she joined him in his office.

"Hi ya..." She called out cheerfully, "...I've got something for you." From her handbag she pulled out a charm of some kind on a woven necklace, "...It's for luck. It was my mother's and you have to wear it." She knew he wouldn't be too impressed, he had no time for mumbo-jumbo stuff, but he was actually far more pleased than she thought. She had told him so little about her mother and father, except that they were dead, and he was pleased that she wanted to give him something so personal.

They left shortly afterwards, telling Cyndy that they were going for some lunch together. The bookshop was still closed and so they had to knock and wait. Susan peered through the dusty windows; the dimly lit interior with its rows and rows of well-worn books filled her with a sudden and unwelcome memory. She pictured her father's study and remembered when, as a child, she would sneak in when he wasn't there and explore his fantastic collection of artefacts. Books, of course, lined the walls, mechanical toys and puzzles lay on the lower shelving, and a free-standing globe beckoned by the window overlooking the garden. Often she would fall asleep under his desk, surrounded by her cache of collected objects, later to be gently roused with a smiling reprove. She shook her head to clear it of emotional baggage.

"Here he comes." She watched Walther appear out

31

of the gloom, looking very much as Richard had described, except perhaps even taller and thinner. He unlocked the door and beckoned them in,

"Thank you for coming, would you follow me through please?" He locked the door behind them and led them to the little room at the back.

"This is my wife; Susan." Walther offered his hand in a polite shake. Seeming ill at ease, he turned to Richard,

"Have you told your wife any of the matters we discussed last evening?"

"Everything." Walther gritted his teeth in frustration and annoyance, turned away for a moment, then whirled on Richard,

"You are a fool! Do you not see the danger of this situation? You have no right to involve other people!" Richard never liked to be shouted at, but before he retorted Susan jumped in,

"If my husband's in danger then I want to know about it! That's my right, and I'm going to be beside him all the way. So stop talking across me as if I'm not here and start talking about what we're supposed to do. Together!" Walther broke the ensuing silence with icy graciousness,

"Please accept my apologies for my outburst. I am a little, um, distracted, at the moment. I have to see to certain arrangements." He was evidently annoyed but at the same time seemed quietly desperate,

"Richard, do you have the address that you promised?" Richard handed over a slip of paper before Susan could stop him; she guessed what Walther would say next,

"Thank you. What there is to be done is for me to do alone. I will trouble you no further. Please leave now, I have much business to attend." His tone was coldly dismissive.

Susan wasn't about to be fobbed off and reared up,

"Oh no you don't! We've got a friend in trouble and we're-" Richard grabbed her lightly on the arm,

"Hold on Sue..." He faced Walther down, "...The police, I'm sure they would be interested in the whereabouts of the so-called New Ripper, don't you think?" He had Walther by the balls and he knew it. Susan grinned; her own wicked lop-sided 'Gotcha' grin,

"Well?" She demanded. Walther sat down wearily behind the desk;

"You must not be so irresponsible. I beg of you. Please consider this. The police, if they are able to arrest her, a matter that I seriously doubt, will not have sufficient evidence for a trial. She will go to ground again, flee the country no doubt. And you..." He pointed his long forefinger at each of them in turn, "...Will be responsible for the suffering and death of Lord knows how many more innocent victims. Will your conscience bear such a weighty burden?"

It was touché moment. In the silence that followed, Susan sat down, a purposeful look on her face, and motioned for Richard to also take a seat,

"We are already involved." She murmured. Walther seized on her remark instantly,

"Ridiculous, how can you be? In what way? You know next to nothing of-" She stared steadily into his eyes forcing him to break off, and then dropped her bombshell,

"I think she murdered my parents."

Chapter 2
"Your fear is my strength..."

A roadside campfire, England

Shielded from the busy road by a knot of trees, the Asian man, Tsuba by name, once again stared into the glowing remains of his campfire. Earlier, the old hag had staggered drunkenly back into their shared home and means of transport, a converted London bus; she snored loudly in the background but, as ever, it never bothered him. Sitting alone in the dark, breathing in the smoke from certain herbs thrown onto the fire, he succumbed to the warm peaceful feeling and allowed the tiny dancing flames to draw him in.

He saw the world through those flames. Saw it and through it, and saw the people on it. And even though he had faced death and atrocity a thousand times, and killed in his turn, he still loved it and all the people on it. Once again he set his mind free to roam the astral plane, searching, searching for her.

London, Windsor

Susan's revelation knocked Richard for six. He had always, or so he convinced himself, respected her silence when it came to talking about her family, believing that one day she would open up to him. That it came out now, in such unexpected fashion, and on top of everything else, threw him into a state of total confusion. Walther suspected as much and melted into the background. Susan stared into Richard's eyes, an imploring look, begging for

35

understanding. They all jumped when the telephone rang. Walther picked it up,

"Walther Von Vohberg speaking."

His conversation was brief and it was obviously to do with his father's funeral, after he had finished the call he turned back to them, his voice weary with sadness,

"Please, I am very busy, perhaps you could visit me tonight? On my father's boat?" Richard looked to Susan for confirmation, she nodded,

"Yes, good idea."

Walther wrote down the address and showed them out politely,

"At seven? I will prepare a little dinner."

"No please, don't go to any trouble."

"It will be no trouble. I look forward to not dining alone for a change."

They left him at the shop door and made their way back to the office,

"I just want to see that everything is okay, then I'll take the rest of the day off." Richard called out, peering round the print-room door looking for Philip.

"He's gone again..." Cyndy announced, "...Finished those books, and then just took off. Says he'll be back tomorrow."

Richard pounded the door in frustration;

"Damn it what the hell is he up to?" He mused aloud and Cyndy picked up on it,

"I don't know Rich, but, well..." She hesitated for a second, "...I'm worried about him. You know how he gets when he meets a girl." Richard knew all right, Phil always fell head-first for the wrong girl, and they always ended up hurting him. He sighed, feeling helpless, remembering the last one,

"Let's just hope he doesn't get hurt like the last time."

London, Windsor

Richard took Susan to lunch in a nearby café, one of those old-fashioned tea-rooms popular with tourists and old people. They got the last vacant table. He had a hundred questions to ask but it was Susan who initiated the conversation,

"I'm sorry Rich, for springing it on you like that. I suppose you're pretty pissed off about it, but I, well..." She dried up, still unable to open up to her husband. They sipped at coffees and picked at toasted sandwiches, quietly incommunicado.

Richard was an orphan, fostered around several times during his childhood. His last 'parents' were by now quite elderly and he rarely visited them, they were just old people to him. Philip Leach had been his anchor during his teenage years, keeping him from going too far off the rails, and when he met Susan she opened his mind to love, she became everything and everyone to him. But he didn't talk about his past, his childhood, and neither did she. They were two broken people thrown overboard and clinging to each other for survival. He realised with a sickening feeling that he might be losing the only two people who ever meant anything to him. It was too painful to dwell on, he blocked the thoughts, closed down his mind to focus on the mundane,

"Maybe I'd better get back to the office..." He eventually suggested, "...Meet you at home later."

"Yes all right then." Their conversation at a complete standstill.

The house in the Countryside ~ 2000

Cairo stepped out suddenly from the dark beside a large wooden wardrobe, a black cross on her ragged white frock, a shadow cast from the attic window. She moved silently to the iron-framed bed against one wall and lay down. Apart from herself, the bed and the wardrobe, the unused attic room was completely empty.

Wind whistled through the trees outside and she wondered what it would be like to go outside, beyond the garden, far away to somewhere else. She imagined a city teeming with cars and people, but had no concept of the poverty, noise or smells. Her city was a warm, kind metropolis, where people smiled and sold ice cream.

She suddenly shivered in the cold, her breath frosty in the moonlight, her bare feet like blocks of ice. Her ever-present imaginary friends were unhappy,

"It's too cold up here."

"We should go back to your bedroom."

"Go to the kitchen first."

"There might be some cake in the larder." Cairo rose quickly and silently disappeared into the black recess beside the wardrobe.

London, River Thames

At seven o'clock Richard and Susan stood together but slightly apart on the north bank of the river Thames, looking for Walther's boat. It was another clear, cold evening; Susan shivered slightly at the sight of the silver moon reflected in the black water. The riverbank was only dimly lit by the occasional lantern making it difficult to see the boat names,

"There it is." Richard pointed to a bulky old-fashioned brown timber houseboat, Persephone printed in faded gold on its stern.

"Watch out for the puddle!" The curtains were drawn, Richard stepped aboard the dark planking at the rear and held out his hand to help Susan, they both turned as the cabin door opened with a rush of warm air and bright cheerful light. Walther's voice called out to them,

"Come in, come in, it is cold this evening." They stepped down into the cabin, squinting as their eyes adjusted to the bright light.

"Welcome to my temporary home..." Walther greeted them warmly as he helped them off with their jackets, "...It was father's pride and joy, this old boat. And now it has come down to me." Richard and Susan looked around in surprise, the décor was magnificent. Panelled end-to-end in walnut and brass, cupboards and shelves all built-in with ornate architraves and beading. Pretty tapestry curtains, each one different but complementing the next, hung on brass poles over the windows. From a drop-down cupboard Walther produced a crystal decanter of ruby wine and motioned for them to sit on a small but comfy sofa near the warmly flickering gas fire. The aroma of peppers and onion wafted through from the galley, Susan suddenly realised that she was ravenous. Walther sat himself on a leather footstool,

"I would like to apologise for my rudeness this morning, I make no excuses, and I must also confess that I cannot remember if I mentioned providing dinner. And so, in order to be on the safe side, I have prepared something." The 'prepared something' turned out to be a fabulously tasty Hungarian goulash served with salad and bread.

39

Richard and Susan ate well, the combination of food, wine and the warm cabin lulling them into a dreamy, relaxed mood. Walther's conversation was quiet but witty and they hardly noticed the passage of time, it was nearly ten o'clock before they got on to the subject of committing murder.

"I still don't understand why we can't just tell the police." Richard stated in exasperation,

"We could even do it anonymously." He added. Walther stared at him for a few moments as if coming to a decision, when he replied his words were clipped, impatient,

"If you inform the police she will escape, I guarantee it. She will then continue to carry out her atrocities elsewhere. She is clever and cautious; do not be under any illusions about her ability to outwit us." He paused briefly before again wagging his finger,

"As I have said, you do not have to be involved." Richard, silenced, looked down into his glass, shaking his head slightly. It was Susan, red in the face, who blurted out,

"I'm in!..." She wagged her own finger back at Walther, "...And don't think that anything you can say will talk me out of it!" Walther sat back quickly, not betraying any emotion but steepling his fingers as if to encourage her to say more, allowing her to continue unchallenged,

"I believe everything you've said, even the crazy stuff, and I agree that the police would be a waste of time. I want to be a part of this, I think I owe it to my parents." Her last few words were spoken more quietly but there was no mistaking the determination in her voice, she wanted in. Richard shook his head again, looking lost and almost helpless for a second, then with an ironic smile he reached out for her,

"Well, I'll try anything once; even murder I suppose." He tried to be flippant but despite this all three of them nodded, satisfied that a commitment was made. Walther cleared his throat quietly before addressing Susan with a level gaze,

"Susan, I do not wish to be impolite, but it might be of some help to our cause if you were to tell me the facts behind your parents, er, untimely, er, well what happened to them?" Richard wasn't prepared for that,

"Oh no, hold on a minute, She's not ready to make th~"

"Rich..." She put up a hand, "...It's okay, I think it's about time I got this off my chest anyway. And besides, having someone else, someone who might not be so sceptical, no offence, to tell it to, might make it a little easier..." They exchanged looks before she continued. "... Forgive me if I ramble a little, I've never told this before, and it was ten years ago..." She took a deep breath and sat back in her seat, "...They were in South Africa on a kind of working holiday, doing research on a book they were writing together. It was a study on the legends of the undead, you know the sort of thing, vampires and zombies and stuff. They claimed that they had some evidence that would prove the legends were based on fact..." Walther leaned forward as she continued, "...I was at university and not really interested, I didn't keep in touch much in those days." They could hear the regret and guilt in her voice, "... Well one day my mother phoned sounding very excited, she said that they had visited a man, a witch doctor I think, who was living with a devil-woman hundreds of years old. Of course I laughed and wished her the best of luck." She paused in her narrative, eyes sparkling. It was clear she found the memories painful, Richard felt compelled to

41

speak,

"It's all right Sue, you don't have to go on if you don't want to." To his annoyance Walther disagreed,

"On the contrary Richard, I believe that Susan will be very glad to finally unburden herself. Is that not so?" He addressed the last remark directly to her, she nodded in agreement and continued,

"I was quite young, I never dreamed anything bad would happen to them. Anyway I wasn't paying too much attention to what mum was saying, I remember I moaned about not having enough money and stuff like that, but I do remember that she briefly described them to me. She said that he was a big African, leader of some tribe or cult, while the woman was white, that struck me as surprising at the time, I don't know why, and apparently the woman was exquisitely beautiful and her name was Raven but she was known as Madame Raven..." She paused and they all heard the bubbling of the coffee percolator from the galley.

Walther rose quietly and made liqueur coffees while she continued, "...Well basically that was the last time I ever spoke to my mother..." Her face, already a mask of emotional pain, hardened even further, "...I got a message some days later saying she was dead and that dad was critical in some hospital or other. After that everything happened in a kind of haze, I was in shock for months. I flew down to be with dad and had to identify mum's body. What was left of it..." Her lips trembled, "...She had been mutilated-" She choked back a sob, "...I had to bury her there, dad was too ill to travel home..." She finally broke, the tears rolled down her cheeks in hot wet streams. Richard also found it difficult to hold back his own tears as she continued, "...Dad never fully recovered, I got him home and had to drop out of Uni to look after him. He died six

42

months later..." Her breathing was in ragged jerks as she tried to hold back her tears, "...Mad and deliriously drunk most of the time. After he'd gone I left the family home, I, I, just locked the door and never went back. It still belongs to me, but I don't know what sort of state it's in. All their research is still there. But don't ask me to go and get it. I couldn't do it." She finally stopped, unable to continue, shaking with desperate sobs. Richard held her close for a few moments until Walther spoke quietly,

"Perhaps we should conclude at this point and meet again tomorrow, yes?" They nodded their agreement, grateful for the chance to leave.

London, Hammersmith

Earlier that same evening, while Richard and Susan were enjoying Walther's goulash, girl-shy Philip Leach sat in Raven's boudoir vigorously sipping wine. She was over-compensating for her depression by drinking and flirting with him.

To his shame he had naively mistaken her flirtatious manner for something more, and now sat red-faced after she had slapped him. She felt his discomfort, enjoyed it, and played with him a little,

"I'm sorry if I gave you the wrong impression..." She gave him an apologetic smile, "...It is just my continental way..." She stood before him and leaned down, "...We can be very, er, touchy-feely..." She drew him up from the seat, "... And kiss each other all the time..." She kissed him lightly on both cheeks, "... But this is not how we kiss in the heat of passion..." She pushed his empty wine glass aside and pressed her lips to his, her body fitting snugly against him from her toes to her breasts, "...We do it like this." The kiss

43

was long and wonderful. Philip, confused as he was, let his arms encircle her as the embrace continued. Eventually Raven peeled away, slightly exhilarated by Philip's runaway passion for her. Thinking that she'd teased him enough, it was time to let him go.

And then he dropped the wine glass. A small thing to lose your life over. It shattered into many crystal fragments. In his embarrassed haste to retrieve the pieces he sliced a deep cut into his middle finger,

"Yow!" He hissed. The pain was sharp. And it hit Raven like a needle to a junkie. Her false playful smile fell away forgotten, she was ravenous. She reached out for his hand, he offered it, she held him by the wrist, and jammed her fingernail into the gash. Philip yelled in shock and pain, trying to withdraw. She held his wrist tightly, the dominatrix awakened,

"You've been a naughty boy..." She reveled in his pain, "...And you must be punished." A huge wave emanated from Philip's confused mind, she quivered, and her smile returned.

In an instant she spun him around and threw him down on his face in the broken glass. In another second she had his arm twisted behind his back as she reached between her legs for her dagger. Philip was scared and yelling, his head twisted to one side. She spoke quickly into his ear, each word as cold and jagged as the broken glass,

"Shut up or I will slit your throat." She pressed the knife point to the side of an eye, Philip's shouts fell to whimpering. In moments she had cut away pieces of his shirt, some she jammed into his mouth, a longer piece she used to secure his hands behind his back. Minutes later the discomfort of his cut finger paled beneath the agonies she put him through as he endured the last moments of his life.

Towards the end of his ordeal he realised that she was actually getting off on his torment. Each agony he suffered brought her closer to some sort of climax, he knew he was doomed. The realisation brought little comfort as he screamed his way into oblivion.

Disposal of his remains was easy. Once she was sated, Raven summoned the twins Margaret and Philippa, the mad, bastard offspring of the housemaid and Sir Clive, the results of a careless fling more than twenty five years ago. They arrived, black plastic sacks at the ready, bickering as usual,

"You chose Tiramisu last night, so now it's my turn to choose!" They stuffed Philip's gory remains into the sacks and lugged him down to the Victorian cellar, then returned upstairs to clean Raven's boudoir. Later, with kitchen knives and saws, they took his body to pieces. Working through the night they drained his blood into the bath and cut him into manageable chunks, finally disposing of him in four weighted sacks dropped from Hammersmith Bridge.

As usual, Raven had been very careful to leave little or no evidence that might connect her to Philip. She'd instructed Franco to move Philip's car to a pub several miles away and there were no records of her at the office; she was quite certain of that, having 'asked' Philip while he was under the knife. He would be reported as 'missing', the absence of a body relegating the police inquiry, 'missing' being not nearly as serious as 'murdered'.

On his return, Franco reported that he'd left Philip's coat in a pub as she'd ordered,

"Thank you Franco." She favoured him with a warm smile as he bowed and turned to go, his old but still firm features as inscrutable as ever. Unconsciously her mind slipped back through the years to 1937. When he was a homeless beggar-child on the ruined streets of Guernica,

"You were such a brave, handsome boy." She whispered to his departing broad shoulders.

She remembered how, as Raven Navaja, she'd been fighting on the side of the Nationalists and entered the city just days after the German bombers had leveled it, the fires still raged, paled only by the fire she saw smouldering in Franco's youthful eyes. He had saved her life, dragged her to safety from an ambush attack.

She took him into her care, to fight alongside her and the Nationalists. He learned the skills of war quickly, and found killing an easy way to channel his anger. He went from small boy to man with nothing in between. Once the revolution was done they settled for a while in Madrid. Raven insisted on his catching up with some schooling while she polished his education in every other way. The Second World War split then up for a time, Raven drawn to the misery of northern Europe like a moth to a flame. But Franco always knew she would return. And when she did, it was to give him the best best time of his life. For years they were inseparable, but further heartbreak was to come to him. She left him again in the 1960's, this time drawn to the horrors in the east. He heard nothing from her for so long that he knew it was over. And so he was surprised when she returned, as beautiful and deadly as the day she left, and pregnant with Cairo. This time she was so very different. So much younger, but in truth it was simply he who now was so much older. Their relationship had become like mistress and servant. He became her bodyguard, on oath to preserve her secrets.

During his life he had made love to her first as a child, then her lover, then as a devoted servant. They trusted each other implicitly, and no one else.

"Franco?" She called after him, very quietly, and was surprised when he stopped and turned, his old and lined face weary but not weak,

"Yes mistress?" She held his gaze for a fleeting second,

"Come..." She asked gently, "...Play with me." And gestured elegantly towards the chess table. He was pleased to join her, and to the accompaniment of Barbieri's opera music they played throughout the night.

London, Windsor

On their way home from Walther's houseboat Susan felt the old insecurities rise up again; washing over and through her, the worthlessness, that vile impotence. How could she express her guilt? How could she ever be worthy of anyone's love? Had she any to give?

"Poor Richard..." She regretted. *"...Do I really love him? Does he love me?"*

They talked little on their way home, neither noticing the passing cars or the piercing crescent moon.

In her mind she whirled and swooped around in a world of regret and guilt.

While his mind was lost in confusion, *"What the hell is going on?"* He tried to rationalise the bizarre twists in recent days. He held on to her arm, caring and wanting her close, and completely unaware that she was oblivious to his touch.

Neither of them heard the enthusiastic shrieking of the teenagers that they crossed the road to avoid, or even the begging whine of the homeless door-sitter. Susan was solely focused on the death of her mother and father, and

47

the role that the strange woman called Raven might have had in it,

"I'll find you." She whispered without realising. Her unconscious words went unnoticed by Richard, drowned out not just by the hubbub as they walked by the open door of a pub, but more by the labyrinthine suppositions whirling around his mind.

At home, like automatons they prepared for bed. Each unconsciously observing their usual bedtime rituals, neither totally aware of each other. Dreams came to both of them, at least they *thought* they were dreams.

Richards dream:

He awoke, stared at the slightly fluttering curtains ahead,

"Why are they red?" his confusion multiplied as they began to part, pulled aside like cinema drapes.

A terracotta-paved street stretched away from him, heat blasted up from the sun-baked stones. He turned suddenly at the sight of buildings to his right, ancient stone crafted and temple-like,

"Is this Rome?" He walked towards the largest temple and passed between the columns, into the grunting melee of an orgy. Men and women of all ages indulged themselves shamelessly, in pairs and in groups, switching from one to another. As he watched he realised that there was one girl in particular that everybody had to have. As if she was an offering to them all. A pretty dark-haired child, obviously not of age. She accepted it all as if resigned to her fate. Except for her green eyes that shrieked of revenge. Throughout her ordeal, he noticed, her piercing hate-filled eyes never strayed far from the man on the gilded couch who seemed to be orchestrating her

48

defilement. Soul stealer.

To his confusion Richard felt himself propelled, by unseen hands, towards the girl, as if it was now his turn,

"Do with her as you wish." The voice came from the man on the gilded couch.

Richard woke as Susan slapped his face, the bedroom came back. She knelt on the bed next to him, the quilt on the floor, she seemed annoyed,

"Sorry Rich, but I had to wake you. You were moaning so loud.

"Shit, I'm glad you did."

"Was it the same as last time?" He didn't want to tell her the contents of the dream,

"Yeah, sort of, it's faded already." Once again he lied and said that he could not remember what the dream was about.

Susan didn't mention that she had had a dream of her own. She had dreamt of a castle in a forest. A castle inhabited by a black beast, it bellowed her name from high windows while she stared from the safety of the trees. She had woken quickly and had lain awake listening to Richard's increasingly noisy slumbering.

The following morning, before they got out of bed, Richard phoned Phil,

"No answer." He hung up, despondent. Susan announced,

"I'm going to phone in sick..." She lay on her back, not facing Richard, "...And I'm going in to work with you, I need to know that Phil's okay and I'd like to be around if Walther shows up." Richard readily agreed, he was deeply rattled. He hoped that Phil had simply gone into work very early, but he doubted it.

They drove to work, aware that they might need the car later on, and arrived at around 7:45. No sign of Phil. They waited nervously, sipping coffee. Cyndy arrived breathlessly as usual at 8.50. By 9.15 they were back in the car heading towards Phil's house in Maidenhead,

"He's dead isn't he?" Susan made the question sound like a statement. Richard couldn't reply, fast losing his patience with the stop-start traffic and his own mounting dread. They saw immediately that Phil's car wasn't in its usual spot on the driveway. Richard was out of the car in a second and almost running to the front door. Susan held back, watching him, knowing he was about to lose his cool. He rang the bell and hammered to no avail,

"Let's try around the back, he might be in the garden." She dutifully followed him through the wrought iron gate and across the crazy paving, aware that it was a preposterous notion but allowing him the moment of action. Of course there was no answer. Richard eventually punched the door one last time and abruptly stopped,

"She's got him." He muttered through clenched teeth. Susan took his arm and started to lead him back towards the car,

"Let's go and find Walther, he'll know what to do." Richard turned on her angrily,

"Fuck him, I'm going to the police! It's what I should've done in the first place, we're crazy thinking we can go up against some kind of fucking mutant psycho. We'll all end up-" Susan put a finger to his lips,

"No Rich, not yet. We have to speak to Walther first..." She opened the car door and sat him on the passenger seat, "...We'll go to his boat and wait for him if necessary." Richard sat quietly while she drove, an angry determination growing within his mind. Mental pictures flashed inside his eyes, pictures like the cruelly rendered bodies in the little book, only this time with Phil's face on them, *"You won't get away with this. I'll get you..."* He thought, realising that maybe it wasn't a job for the police at all, *"...No, it's down to me. You were my friend, my mate."* An unexpected tear appeared at the corner of his left eye, he wiped it away before Susan could notice. She looked at him a second later, a grim smile before she turned her eyes back to the road.

It was a grey noon when they reached the boat, Walther came stooping out of his cabin to greet them as they arrived on deck,

"I am just preparing coffee." They could hear the cheerfully bubbling percolator as they descended into the luxurious room. Minutes later Susan had related their story, Richard ominously silent, Walther nodded and shook his head appropriately,

"I am sorry, I am afraid we shall have to assume the worst consequence..." He paused only for a moment, "...I believe your friend to be dead. It would be most uncharacteristic if he were to now turn up safe and well." Richard glared at Walther as if he somehow blamed him, Susan watched uneasily, well aware how difficult to handle Richard could be when he lost it. Even she was surprised when he spoke, so bitter and angry were his words,

"So just how and when are going to kill this fucking bitch?"

Walther raised an aristocratic eyebrow and a finger to his chin before making his reply,

"Tomorrow is my father's funeral, at 10:00..." Both Richard and Susan cursed themselves for insensitivity as Walther continued, "...I have drawn up a plan for the

51

execution of the Raven creature…" His voice did not hide his annoyance at their lack of propriety, "…I suggest we meet as soon after the ceremony as I see fit to discuss it. Do I have your agreement?" They nodded, although Richard a little absently. Susan again took his arm,

"We should go…" She smiled apologetically at Walther and led Richard out, "…Come on, let's go home."

They spent the rest of the day at home, Richard restless and irritable. He kept going on about wanting to do something, but when Susan dared ask,

"Such as?" He became furious and threw things around,

"I don't fucking know; all right!" He screamed. Eventually she went to bed,

"Good night." Richard ignored her and opened another bottle of wine. She pretended to be asleep when he eventually stumbled into their bedroom, hoping that he would be better in the morning.

The house in the Countryside ~ 2000

The twins Philippa and Margaret, or Pip and Emm as they were more commonly known, lay comfortably together in each other's arms. They took solace in each other for the yearning of a lover. They had known men; at least, that is, they had been used by their father, Sir Clive. It was not the physical act that so absorbed them, but the almost inconceivable notion that there could be another form of love. They had read magazines and watched soap operas, and at twenty five years old love was something they craved.

Their mother, the housekeeper, had been aware of their incestuous cuddling and had not appeared to disapprove. Nor had she interfered when at nine years old, during one of Raven's long absences, they were ravaged by the selfish and beastly Sir Clive. Their lives had been woven by violence and violent sex. They knew of other ways to express love, or lust, but had no experience. Oddly though, they were content, happy even, with their bizarre and extreme existence, awe-filled and worshipful of their goddess, Raven. To them she was everything a woman should aspire to be, strong, proud and beautiful. Unlike the petty and shallow whinger, Sir Clive. They were always sad that Raven spent so much of her time elsewhere, dining with princes in exotic palaces they presumed.

Their mother was a disappointment; they thought her weak and careless, knowing nothing of the years of relentless repression heaped upon her by her 'master'. And never, even as infants had they been allowed to see the scars of his interest on her once smooth skin. In truth, most people they knew were a disappointment to them, why were they not as beautiful and glamorous as the idols they worshipped on the television?

"It's our birthday soon..." Whispered Emm conspiratorially, "...What shall we have?" Her eyes sparkled and there was a brief pause before they announced together,

"New dresses!" They laughed and hugged each other, happy in their snug world of the insane.

*

Raven lounged on a sofa, barely dressed but caring not at all, the television flickered in her eyes; or was it the flicker of hate and loathing for everything she saw? Languidly she reached for the cord that rang the bell to

53

summon Franco.

He had been made to be alone. But it was far more than loneliness that had ailed him. His family quite literally blown to pieces. He hated the bombers that smashed and burned, and destroyed. And he hated the rest of the world for allowing it to happen. As a suddenly orphaned child he had hated everything and everyone, choosing to fight any who would get in his way. and he would make them all pay, in time. And then as the years went by his hate evolved into a disgust for humanity, and contempt for its foibles. But for Raven he felt different. She had cared for him, devoted herself strangely and unstintingly to him throughout the years, the bond had never wavered. She was his family. Never would he be able to betray her. The bell rang. He appeared within moments,

"Yes Mistress?" She smiled at his entrance, obedient yes, but never subservient,

"We're going out." She announced with a glint in her eye. Franco smiled slightly and nodded,

"As you wish Mistress."

London, Windsor

Richard muttered as he and Susan sat nursing cups of strong coffee,

"I just don't think I could handle a funeral right now." Once again they had slept badly and risen early, it was nearly nine and Walther's father's funeral was at ten. Susan nodded and offered the coffee pot for a refill,

"Why don't you just go to work, I'll go to the funeral with Walther; we could meet you later." He was grateful for the let-off, it was Saturday morning and he would be alone at the office where he could get some serious

54

thinking done. A few minutes later they left in separate cars; having arranged to meet at Walther's boat at one o'clock.

Richard let himself into the office and stood for a few moments on the threshold just looking in. It was cold and silent, just as he knew it would be. But believing, knowing, that Philip was gone forever made it seem desolate. Eventually he closed the door, went in and sat in Cyndy's swivel chair. From there he could see all of reception and the doors to his and Philip's offices. His bottled up emotions had started to get the better of him. Frustration turned to anger and then to rage. He opened a drawer for no reason and slammed it shut, only to open it again a second later. He'd seen the corner of an invoice. An invoice with   no name on it but there was the Hammersmith address, he carefully picked it out of the drawer and laid it out on the desk in front of him. He knew it was the invoice for Raven's ghastly books and for a short while he just stared at it, twiddling with a pencil in one hand, Cyndy's letter opener in the other. Eventually the pencil snapped in half, it was the moment that Richard came to a decision,

"I'm going to get that fucking bitch!" He muttered to himself as he left the office at a run, the letter opener still clutched tight in his left hand.

London, river Thames

Walther was standing on the small deck at the rear of his boat as Susan drove up. He wore an immaculate dark charcoal suit and in the pale morning light his tall gaunt frame appeared fragile and lonely,

"Ahoy there!" Susan called out as she locked her car,

55

she smiled and he helped her to clamber aboard.

She noticed his long fingers were freezing cold and assumed he had been stood outside for some time.

"Richard sends his apologies." She meant to elaborate further but Walther held up a hand and interrupted,

"There is no need for apologies, I understand. Believe me. But we are in need of some haste, I do not wish to be late on such an occasion. May I suggest we share my car?" He waved towards a row of timber garages on the other side of the quay. Susan shrugged,

"Yes, whatever. I'm easy." Without further comment he strode across to a black painted wooden door, took some keys from his pocket and removed the chunky padlock, she dragged open one door while he did the other, a small smile spread across his face as the car was revealed,

"Father's **other** pride and joy." Susan waited outside as he forced himself into the 1961 E-type Jaguar. The engine started at the third attempt and he inched the car out into the daylight,

"He bought it from the showroom..." He called out to her, "...drive yours inside, it will be safer there." She nodded and drove her car into the dark garage, parking with the passenger side as close as she dared to the wall.

He smiled thinly as he closed the garage doors, and made sure the padlock was back on tight. In the open air of the quayside Susan felt a moment of embarrassment as he opened the E-type's door for her,

"Thank you." She murmured as she settled into the low seat.

The drive was pretty much stop-start as they crawled through traffic, conversation was limited until Susan remembered something Richard had told her,

"Richard told me your father was in the Resistance?"

"Yes, towards the end of the war he escaped servitude under the Nazis, I believe it was there that he met Raven."

"Do you think she would've helped him?"

"Why on earth would you think that? She is a monster."

"I don't know…" Susan frowned, shaking her head, "…I really don't know why I said that." She changed the subject,

"Richard also said you have an older brother, will he be at the funeral?"

"Erm yes, he will, he has flown over."

"Younger or older?"

"What?"

"Your bother, is he younger or older than you?" Walther seemed a little put-out by the questions but replied readily enough,

"He is older, several years older…" He paused while turning a corner, "…His name is Henrik. He was born just after the war."

"Oh? Just after the war." She said, while in her mind she thought, *"So he was conceived while your father was in the Resistance."*

London, Hammersmith

Richard got into his car, hands shaking so violently he could barely insert the key, once the engine started he gripped the wheel tightly in both hands in an effort to calm his racing nerves. Taking a deep breath he 'switched off' his racing mind, a skill he'd practised since a teenager enabling him to appear calm under the most stressful of

57

conditions. As he drove towards London he tried to picture what he might do if he found Raven at the address, it had already occurred to him that it could likely be a false address and that he was on a wild-goose chase. If, however, she was there, could he kill her as Walther had insisted? He reached into his jacket pocket and pulled out the paper-knife, it was light and blunt but he felt sure it could still take a life. At a set of traffic lights in the Hammersmith area he fumbled through the glove compartment for his A–Z street guide. He found the street easily enough and quickly pulled into a parking space vacated by a delivery van. The house was several doors behind on the same side, a large three-storey brick terrace, well maintained with a short flight of steps leading up to an imposing door with shiny brass furniture. He sat and watched for a few minutes through his wing mirror while he built himself up, *"Stay calm, but break the fucking door down if they won't let you in..."* With deliberate deep breaths he got out of the car, locked the door, walked up the street and climbed the steps, *"...And if they call the police to arrest me – good! At least it will prove that Walther's story is a load of bollocks."* He grabbed the large brass knocker immediately in his right hand and banged it hard several times.

He waited in a kind of trance, with no idea what to expect, and no clear idea of what he was going to do. A few moments later a small middle-aged woman with hostile lips and defeated eyes greeted him,

"Can I help you?" Her tone said more than her words, she would give him about two seconds, he knew he had to push it,

"I'm here to see, her." He knew he sounded stupid.

"Is it business?" She snapped, half closing the door.

"Yes! It, It's about those books." She closed the door even further,

"Have you got an appointment?" Without thinking, Richard stepped forward and pushed the door, sent the small woman staggering back,

"How dare you!" She screamed at him, eyes like slits. He stepped further inside,

"Just go and tell her the man from B & L printers is here, she'll see me!" Instead of scurrying off as he'd hoped, the woman stood her ground, folded her arms firmly across her chest and waited as if something was about to happen. It was at that moment that Richard saw Franco coming down the stairs with a frown of zero tolerance etched across his brow, *"Oh shit!"* Richard braced himself for a fight.

London, River Thames

Susan was surprised that the funeral was not a more sombre affair. There had been a large gathering of mourners at the graveside and mostly they chatted and exchanged greetings like old friends,

"Father had a great many friends." Afterwards at a small reception in a nearby hotel there was a mountain of cards and flowers from friends and relatives abroad. Walther introduced her as a friend and she was greeted cordially. Walther had asked that the mourners come together in a celebration of his father's life rather than grieving his death, and as such had asked several of them to relate one story or event that typified his colourful life. The time passed quickly during the engrossing tales and she almost regretted having to leave before they were all told. Walther made their apologies,

"We have another very pressing engagement." They

arrived back at the boat at ten past one, swapped their cars around in the shabby wooden garage and stood on the riverbank for a while waiting for Richard. The weather had turned gloomy and overcast and a light drizzle had begun to fall.

"We should wait inside." Walther suggested. She nodded in agreement adding,

"Can I use your phone?" As he unlocked the cabin door,

"Of course." He politely busied himself in the galley as she dialled Richard's office number, the answer phone came on which meant that he had left already, so she expected him to arrive at any moment. By one forty five she started to worry,

"He should have been here ages ago." She fretted and fiddled with the empty coffee cup on her lap.

London, Hammersmith

"Is there a problem Joan?" Franco asked while maintaining constant eye contact with Richard, staring with a terrifying intensity. Joan's voice was high with victory,

"It's this man. He has no appointment but he will not leave..." Her left eyebrow rose as a smug smile creased her thin lips, "...And he assaulted me!"

In desperation, Richard reached inside his jacket for the invoice. It was, to Franco, a threatening move, and he flashed forward grabbing Richard's arm and spinning him around as the invoice fluttered to the floor in front of Joan. She picked it up, instantly recognising its significance as Franco frog-marched Richard out through the door,

"Wait!..." She called out, "...bring him back." Adding

in a quieter tone, "...He knows about Sir Clive's books." Franco dutifully marched Richard back in, his frown much deepened at the mention of Sir Clive. Joan hurriedly closed the door while Richard was bundled into a timber-floored reception room, from the corner of an eye he saw the slim shape of Raven, smiling and beguiling, provocatively draped across a large sofa. For a few moments nobody spoke, as if it was impolite to speak before the Mistress. Richard was forced into a chair and motioned to keep still with Franco poised above him. He realised with blinding conviction how stupid he'd been in trying to tackle Raven alone, he stared at her, noticing her extraordinariness. Beautiful, but not in a cover-girl way, something more timeless. Her eyes allowed him to look at her, eyes that had seen hell and no longer cared,

"You are Richard, yes?" She had broken the silence and so Joan felt free to tell what had happened,

"He just barged in-" Raven raised a hand,

"That's all right Joan, you may go now." Summarily dismissed, Joan threw a spiteful glare at Richard as she left the room. Raven raised herself gracefully from the sofa,

"Have you searched him?"

"Yes Mistress." Richard hadn't even noticed being frisked,

"He carried no proper weapon, just his wallet and this." Franco held out the letter-opener. Her smile broadened,

"Such a deadly weapon, you must have killed a great many people." She mocked him playfully as she undulated across the room to a cocktail cabinet. Richard tried an all too obvious bluff,

"I've told the police where I am, if I go missing they'll be coming after you." She laughed gently as she poured

61

out two crystal goblets of wine,

"And why would they? What have you told them?"

"I told them you killed my friend Philip Leach, and I'm going to see that you pay for it!" Again she laughed, then sighed,

"Here, drink with me. Then I'll explain." She put a glass in his hand, lifted hers to her lips, Richard obeyed without question and drank a large soothing mouthful. She did not. With another slightly more wistful sigh she returned her wine to the decanter. Richard watched in stunned realisation, mortified by his own stupidity,

"Poisoned?" He asked weakly, expecting an imminent painful gut-wrenching death. He was glad that Susan wasn't there to see how pathetic he'd been. And it was that sudden thought, that he would never see her again, that spurred him into a last desperate act, rekindling his anger. He launched himself from the chair, kicking and punching like a madman. He caught Franco slightly off guard and bowled him over. Luck was on his side, he rammed his knee into Franco's groin and the paper knife clattered to the floor. He seized it and advanced on Raven with intent to murder. But his legs had other ideas. The room began to spin and Raven seemed to recede, with gritted teeth he forced his legs forward one short wonky step after another.

"It always gets the legs first." Raven offered the information in a calm matter-of-fact way,

"Then moves up into the hands and body, are you still able to speak?" He tried but no words came out and his breathing became short and laboured, he watched in silent terror as Raven dropped away from him and the floor rushed up towards his face. He went down hard, his face suddenly warm and wet from a bloody nose.

"Turn him over!" He heard Raven's voice through cotton wool ears as Franco's strong hands yanked him over on to his back. There was a sharp pain in his chest,

"Pull it out!" Again he heard Raven's voice from just behind his head, Franco knelt and Richard felt another jolt of pain as the bent and bloody paper knife was tugged from his chest.

"Is the cut deep?" She demanded,

"No mistress, merely a flesh wound, he is in no danger from it." Franco had probed the incision with the tip of the knife. Raven pursed her lips and relished Richard's pain,

"I will dispose of him later." A half smile crossed her lips,

"In the meantime there are things to attend to. I want you to go to his offices, search for anything that might lead the police to us, burn the whole building down if necessary. I will question this one to see if anyone else knows of this address, and there may be a little wifey at home; she will have to be dealt with also. Search him for car keys." Franco went expertly through Richard's pockets and placed all the contents on a small table, Raven smiled at the picture of Susan in his wallet,

"Take his car, go now I want this done as quickly as possible, leave it at his office and return here using the Underground. Report to me on your return, we shall be leaving this house tonight." Franco left with a nod, Richard was surprised to feel the effect of the drug beginning to wear off already and realised that he wasn't about to die after all, Raven stalked around the room like a predatory animal, excited by the waves of pain and anger emanating from him. Richard took a few deep breaths and began to calm himself, he relaxed his mind and stepped back from

63

the pain. Raven whirled on him like an angry cat,

"What are you doing?" She hissed. Richard shrugged in confusion, it was some seconds before he remembered Walther's words *"they feed on the brain 'waves' of others"* and realised that he had won a tiny victory, a small ironic grin half broke out on his face; quickly turning into a grimace as she slapped him hard across the cheek,

"I control your pain. Think on it. Before long you will be screaming for mercy like all the rest." She left the room as the twins arrived, giggling as usual, something that always irritated Raven,

"Stop that stupid giggling and get that mess cleared up!" She waved to indicate that Richard was the 'mess'. Suddenly quiet, they waited while Raven receded along the corridor. With short steps they stopped at Richard's feet and stared, starting at the bottom and taking him all in, pausing at various points of interest. Finally they turned, round eyed, to face each other, their voices solemn,

"This one's for us!"

London, Walther's Houseboat

By three O'clock Susan had become seriously distressed. Walther had been watching her as he busied himself with domestic chores around the boat, they had spoken little and the atmosphere was filled with quiet anticipation, they heard the gentle sounds of the water on the hull and the soft ticking of the clock next to the barometer.

"Something must have happened to him." Susan finally voiced her fear, Walther noticed her eyes sparkling wet, he wanted to offer some words of comfort but found himself merely voicing his own anxieties,

"You do not suppose that Richard would have been so foolish to go after Raven alone?" Susan looked down at her clenched fingers before replying,

"He was very upset, and he is impulsive. But he's not stupid! Surely not, I don't think he would've gone without us." She shook her head, not believing her own words, clawing away a sudden rush of tears down her cheeks. Walther sat next to her and offered a tissue, he felt wretched, wishing with all his heart that he'd never let Richard and Susan become involved. After a few seconds he rose again,

"I should, perhaps, tell you of my plan to execute Raven?" He opened a wooden box as he spoke, Susan nodded for him to go ahead. With a flourish he produced a handgun, a German Luger,

"I will wait outside her 'home' until she appears, then I will shoot her like a dog in the street." She stared him in the eyes for a moment, waiting for something else, he shrugged,

"That's it. A simple plan I confess, but effective I believe." With a catch in her voice she asked,

"That's it? The great plan? Shoot her? Well if it's that easy how come no one's done it before?"

Walther was unperturbed,

"You thought perhaps a stake through the heart? No, she is quite mortal, a single head-shot should suffice, although one in the heart also for good measure."

"Not even silver bullets?" Susan seemed desolate at the simplicity of it. Again they lapsed into silence until she asked in a quiet earnest way,

"Will you come with me to look for Richard? Please? I want to check the office and then home. But I don't want to be on my own if there's bad news."

"Yes, of course I will accompany you." They left almost immediately after Walther had restored the Luger to its box. This time they took Susan's car,

"I'll bring you back later." The Saturday afternoon traffic was slow and it was beginning to get dark by the time they neared the office. The drizzle had persisted all afternoon and formed puddles, the windscreen wipers grated across the screen,

"What the hell's that?" Susan pointed at a plume of black smoke rising above the rooftops ahead of them, they turned a corner to find the road ahead blocked by the bulk of a fire appliance, its bright lights flashing. She stopped the car and they both jumped out, somehow they both knew which building was on fire. Walther paused at the hastily erected barrier but Susan ran straight under it and kept running. As she got closer she could see Richard's empty car parked outside the blazing office and immediately assumed he was inside, she stopped dead, transfixed. It was only when a policeman grabbed her by the arm that she found he voice,

"My husband's in there! Let me go dammit!" She struggled with the police officer as he dragged her back towards the barrier, Walther caught up with them halfway back, together with a paramedic from an attending ambulance they tried to calm her down, he also asked the policeman to fetch the senior fire officer.

Susan had become quiet by the time the fire officer arrived, her head down. He spoke in the matter-of-fact way that emergency professionals adopt,

"The blaze was well under way by the time we got here, but I did manage to get a man inside briefly..." Susan looked up quickly as the man continued, "...It looked to him

66

as if the place was empty, I can't guarantee it, but we'll know more in a couple of hours." She listened as if from a distance,

"Thank you..." She murmured absently, "... I'm sure you're right." Her gaze had shifted away from him as he'd spoken and remained fixed on Richard's car. The fire officer could say nothing more and left. Walther sensed that Susan was holding something back,

"What is it? What are you thinking?" He could tell that she knew something that he didn't. She waited until they were out of earshot before replying,

"It's the car, it's Richard's all right, but he didn't park it there. You see, he's got his habits like all of us. He never leaves it facing the wall like that, and especially not in Phil's parking space. He always, and I do mean always, reverses into his spot." Walther nodded in understanding,

"So we are to assume that someone else parked his car, and most likely the same someone set fire to the office, but why?"

They waited for a little over an hour before the all-clear, the building was empty.

"Let me take you home." Walther led her towards the car, opened her door sat her in and closed it for her. Then, after starting the engine, spoke a little apologetically,

"I am sorry, but I do not know where you live. A few directions perhaps?" She could not help but release an ironic smile.

London, Hammersmith

Of course the twins had owned pets before. But this one was going to be different, it was a real living, breathing man. They were ecstatic, somehow in their warped non-sane minds they had decided it would be okay to keep Richard, not exactly as a prisoner, although they knew full well that he must never be allowed to escape. They wanted simply to 'look after' him, to care for him, to love him. And, they hoped, and could see no reason why not, he would also come to love them.

With great effort they dragged his limp and delirious form onto a kitchen chair and handcuffed him to a water pipe, then with much tenderness they washed the blood from his face and hair,

"We shall have to take his clothes off." Said Margaret, the decisive one. Neither of them moved for a little while,

"How?" The other eventually asked. Margaret, known as Emm to her sister, went to a drawer and withdrew a large pair of scissors, carefully she cut along the sleeves of his jacket and shirt until the cuts met in the middle, then from either side they peeled back the blood-soaked garments,

"Look at that!.." Pip pointed to the paper-knife wound in his chest, "...He's still bleeding." Together they leaned forward for a closer inspection,

"It's not too deep, but he needs stitches..." They concurred, "...I'll fetch the sewing kit." Emm left the room at a happy trot.

Richard groggily came to and looked up into Pip's round and staring eyes, she didn't blink but suddenly blurted out,

"You're going to be very happy here." Followed by a frown and a smile. Richard turned at the sound of Emm's return, she carried a large tapestry covered sewing box,

"Here I am." She plonked the box down and threw

open the lid, inside was a jumble of sewing effects,

"Which colour cotton shall we use?" The decision making process took several moments before they decided on blue to match Richard's eyes. They worked carefully on him as he gradually rose to a painful fully consciousness, and were nearly finished when Raven breezed into the room, she spoke immediately,

"What are you doing?" She asked in a level, even, tone. Richard noticed that she had put some clothes on and that she looked quite normal in jeans and sweatshirt. The twins stood up, one on either side of him,

"We want to keep him." They announced, almost but not quite defiantly. Raven smiled, then sighed a little theatrically,

"But my dears you're not very good with pets are you? Remember what happened to the last one?" The girls looked sheepish,

"That wasn't our fault..." They agreed, "...It didn't love us!" It was to them a clear and reasonable excuse. Raven laughed, she realised that it might not be a bad idea to let them keep Richard for a while,

"Very well you can keep him. But you'll have to get him ready to travel, we're leaving this house today. We're going to spend some time in the country, at Sir Clive's estate. And remember this..." She added darkly, holding their attention, "...If he escapes he will bring the police, and they will take you away. They will split you up and put you in different Asylums, do you understand?" The girls nodded gravely. They were afraid of the Asylum, they wouldn't let him escape.

Richard half heard the conversation before he again drifted back into semi-consciousness, the words *"going to the asylum"* on repeat in his mind.

A roadside campfire, England

Tsuba carefully studied the glowing embers, his mind combing the vast expanses of the astral plane. Seeing once again, the girl with the black hair and jade green eyes.

"She is close. I know it." He sprinkled a few more herbs onto the flames and deeply inhaled the ensuing aromatic smoke. Her visage came and went, fleeting but vivid. And recently so near.

"I will find you, never doubt it my beautiful soaring bird..." The smoke made his eyes water, "...And I will hold you in my arms again at last."

Chapter 3
"Your despair is my promise..."

London, Windsor

Susan and Walther were startled awake by the sound of the front door bell. It was 8:30am the next morning, she had slept in the bedroom and Walther had spent the night fully dressed on the sofa. He opened the door as Susan hurriedly wrapped herself in a dressing gown.

"Mr Bryant? Thames Valley Police..." Two plain-clothed officers stood close to the door, "...May we come inside sir?" They brandished I.D. as they stepped inside without waiting for an answer. Susan, looking as if she'd been awake most of the night, joined them in the small hallway,

"Is it about Richard? Have you found him? Is he all right?" Her voice sounding almost desperate. The two officers looked at Walther, then at each other, appearing somewhat puzzled,

"Sorry madam, you've lost us, has he been reported missing?" Then turned to look at Walther who then introduced himself,

"I am Walther Von Vohberg..." He paused for a moment, "...A friend."

They all stood in the hallway with the front door slightly ajar, Susan reddening as she answered the officer's questions,

"He didn't come home last night, Richard, my husband." She spoke guardedly, not willing to mention anything about Raven, it was obvious to the policemen

71

that she was hiding something. They took Walther's name and address and asked him to show some I.D. before continuing to press for information,

"We really came to speak to Mr Bryant about last night's fire, the Fire Brigade have confirmed it was definitely arson..." The policeman spoke with professional authority, "...And Mr Philip Leach, do you know where he is?" Susan's jaw tightened,

"No, sorry." The second policeman raised his eyebrows while the first spoke,

"Are you telling me, Mrs Bryant, that both your husband and his business partner have gone missing, and by coincidence on the very same night that their premises happens to be burned down?" Susan didn't reply, she could easily imagine what they were thinking. For a while none of them spoke, it was the oldest trick used by the police to intimidate a suspect into breaking the silence, in this instance it failed and the officers decided nothing more could be gleaned at the present,

"We shall need a statement off Mr Bryant when he shows up, get him to call me at the station?" She led them to the door,

"Yes. I will..." She feigned a polite smile, "...Thank you." let them out and closed it.

The two officers sat in their car for a few minutes before driving off, not happy with the situation,

"So what do you think's going on then?" The one behind the wheel asked.

"I'm not sure, but my first hunch is that the two blokes, Bryant and Leach, have got themselves mixed up in something they can't handle and done a runner, Porn maybe, or counterfeiting." The other nodded in approval,

"Yes, and they could've burnt down their own

premises in an effort to destroy the evidence." He started the engine

"What about those two in there?..." He nodded towards the house, "...She knows something that she doesn't want to tell us." They both nodded,

"Oh well, let's put in the report and see how it pans out."

Susan came back down the stairs whilst Walther looked out of the front window,

"They're going." He murmured.

"Yes, and so are we, come on." She was dressed, and had decided they were going to call on 22 Old Bridge Street, after stopping off at Walther's boat to collect the gun. She bustled him out of the house without breakfast or even coffee.

The house in the Countryside ~ 2000

Richard regained consciousness in semi-dark on the back seat of a large car, sandwiched between the twins. Franco was driving and Raven sat in the front passenger seat. The drug had worn off leaving Richard in a lot of pain, he groaned and tried to move his arms but found himself handcuffed to the twins' wrists.

"Look Pip, he's awake at last!" Emm declared as she turned to face him,

"We're going to stay in the countryside for a while." A hand pulled his head around to face Pip,

"That'll be nice won't it?" Richard closed his eyes and groaned again,

"Yes delightful." He mumbled ironically. Even with his eyes closed he could still feel them staring adoringly at him, and it occurred to him that if he was ever to find a way

73

out of his predicament it would be with the help of the twins, whether by choice or design. He realised that it might be to his advantage to play along,

"I've always wanted to live in the countryside." He opened his eyes and gave them what he hoped was a friendly smile, they beamed in return. All were quiet for a while and Richard noticed the time on the dashboard, 10:00. A road sign flashed by stating Wallingford 8 miles. Shortly afterwards they turned off the main road into a narrow lane lined by bushes and trees,

"We must be in 'the countryside'." He observed to the delight of the twins.

And sure enough, moments later, a large country house loomed up ahead, lit up by rows of decorative lamp-posts around a circular front lawn. The grand front doors opened as they approached and they were greeted by a surly-looking young man who, somewhat grudgingly, helped Franco with the bags. Raven ordered the twins away to the servants quarters with Richard in tow. They formed a short Conga-chain as they wound their way upstairs, finally climbing a very narrow staircase to the top floor. He was led into a small attic room, with bare floorboards and no other furniture than a single iron-framed bed, small table and a brown wooden wardrobe. Handcuffed by his right wrist to the bedstead they told him to lie down and wait,

"We'll be back soon. We promise!" Emm crossed her heart,

"And we'll bring you some food," Pip added sounding very organised. They were turning to go as Richard dropped a bombshell,

"I need to use the bathroom." Their jaws dropped, neither of them had considered his toilet requirements, and

74

there was the usual short silence before Emm inquired delicately,

"For number one, or number two?"

"Number one." He groaned.

They overcame the problem by providing him with a plastic bucket and some toilet tissue, he heard them giggle as they waited outside for him to finish. They took the bucket away with more giggles and a promise to return with some food, Richard called out to them as they were closing the door,

"Could you get me some painkillers as well?"

With the barmy girls gone the little room was suddenly very cold and empty, he couldn't move away from the bed so he dragged it with him to the small square window. He pushed the sash lever across and struggled to raise the window high enough to put his head out. He guessed that he was at the back of the house, although it was too dark to see clearly. Then he hauled the bed across to the wardrobe and opened the door,

"Empty." He noticed a scuff mark on the floorboards as if the wardrobe had recently been moved away from the wall. He thought about trying to shift it but decided to wait until later, *Those two nutters might be back at any moment.* "He lay down painfully on the narrow bed, just as footsteps heralded the twins return,

"Here we are again!" They marched in, each bearing a laden tray,

"Sandwiches first." Emm proclaimed,

"Then you can have some cake." Pip added.

They placed one tray on the little table and the other on the floor, then they helped him to a sitting position and offered a cheese sandwich. Richard dutifully took it and remembered to smile, asking

"Did you bring the painkillers?" They solemnly shook their heads,

"You mustn't take pills on an empty stomach."

"But I'm eating right now you bloody~" Richard blurted out angrily, stopping himself before he cursed them. And then after silently consulting each other they uttered together,

"We'll bring you some later." The conversation lapsed after that while they gazed saucer-eyed at him eating. When he'd had enough they took up the trays without a word and left.

"He doesn't talk very much!" He heard one complain as they locked the door.

*

Raven sprawled on a chair in front of the television, the News had just shown the latest terrorist arson attack on a London hotel. Franco was on the other side of the room playing computer Chess. She spoke to him,

"Did I ever tell you about that fire I started in London?" She asked the question in a careless kind of way as if she was reminiscing about a day at the seaside.

"No." Was his reply, the tone of which did not particularly invite her to continue. So she did anyway,

"Well, you know that so-called Great fire of London? It was no accident." She waited for a comment that didn't come, then continued,

"Some sickeningly pious Puritan priest had recently cursed me *"I name thee Raven!"* because I'd been carrying on with an old wool merchant, nice enough chap, except to his wife. Well he was quite friendly with Wren and several other vested-interest types, I met them at a party. The engrossing conversation turned to a slum clearance project they'd been trying to get off the ground, they wanted more inner-city space for their grand houses and so on. So in the middle of the conversation I said why don't you just burn it all down and start again! Of course everyone laughed thinking I'd made a good joke. One of them was even stupid enough to say that it would be a good way to get rid of the rats once and for all. Then later in the evening, after more drinks had been consumed, the subject came up again, and this time somebody said the magic words: What if?"

Franco whispered,

"Check."

Raven continued her tale,

"So they hatched a plan, they all knew the city well enough, and there was this Dutch sea-captain who knew all about wind directions and things, so the next big question simply became 'where and when?' Of course I volunteered straight away, as did Wren and the sea captain, although he was more than a bit drunk. The fourth member in our little plot was the doctor, he professed to be acting for 'the greater good of mankind' or some such rubbish.

What a night that was! The chaos, it was fantastic, you could practically walk across the river, there were so many people in it. And the funny thing is, the doctor was right, it was good for the city in the long run. Pity he didn't live to see any of it, such an insufferable do-gooder. I pushed him down a well. Life was so much simpler in those days." She finished her story with a sigh.

"Mate!..." Franco turned to face her, victory on his face, "...What were you saying?" He obviously had barely heard a word, she glared at him for a moment, then turned back to the television.

London, Hammersmith

Susan and Walther hardly spoke a word on their way to Hammersmith, Walther found a parking space and eventually broke the silence,

"I imagine there is little point in me asking you to stay in the car while I go in, is there?" Walther asked, and was a little taken aback at her sharp response,

"No fucking point whatsoever!" Being a little old school he didn't quite approve of women swearing,

"I thought as much." He murmured as he parked the Jaguar as near to the house as possible and quickly got out. She followed him to the shiny black front door. Adrenalin pumped through her, she was shaking and felt slightly sick.

They waited several moments before the door opened revealing a hard-faced middle-aged woman, her mouth opened to speak and Susan was shocked as Walther charged straight in pushing the woman to the floor. In one fluid movement he pulled out the vintage handgun and pointed it at her face,

"Where is Richard Bryant? Where is he?" Walther looked dangerous and determined. Then with exaggerated slowness he pulled back the hammer of the gun. The woman lay flat on the floor, she was scared and her breath came in short gasps, but to Susan's astonishment she turned her head to one side and closed her eyes,

"Never heard of him." She whispered, as if resigned to her death. Walther remained stern,

"Get up!" She opened her eyes and slowly climbed back to her feet, Walther called out to Susan without taking his eyes off the woman,

"Pull her arms behind her back and hold them tight!" She did as she was told and got a firm grip on the woman's arms while Walther continued to question her,

"Who else is in this house?" He kept the pistol aimed at her face, her head shook as she replied,

"No one, there's only me."

"Take us upstairs, I want to see every room in the house!" The woman slowly led them from room to room and it gradually became obvious that the house was indeed, empty. Worse, in a way; was that they saw no sign of Richard ever having been there. Susan became more desperate as they came back downstairs to stand in a comfortable sitting room. She began to twist the older woman's arms painfully,

"Just tell us where my husband is! Then we'll leave you alone!" The woman had been stony faced as she led them around, and broke her silence only to say,

"I don't know what you're talking about." There was a moment of hesitation before Susan snapped,

"Shoot her!" She cried out as she pushed the woman away towards a wall,

"Just do it! She's obviously not going to tell us anything, so just shoot the fucking bitch!" She saw the woman stiffen and begin to tremble.

They were in the room where Richard had fought with Franco, it had been thoroughly cleaned and showed no sign of the struggle, the drugged wine decanter was still on the shelf. Walther motioned for the woman to sit in the chair, she edged to it and sat stiffly, Susan immediately confronted her,

"Why don't you just tell us what we need to know?"

"I can't tell you anything." Without warning Susan slapped her hard across the face, so hard that her hand

79

hurt. The woman was nearly knocked out of the chair, her cheek already turning livid, but still she said nothing. Walther had busied himself by opening drawers and doors in the hope of finding a clue, he quickly realised that it would be a fruitless search. Susan turned to him, shaking, her face white with anger,

"So what do we do now?" She asked him. He shrugged and shook his head,

"I suppose we could wait here. Someone or something might turn up." It wasn't much of a plan but at that moment it was all they'd got. The woman sat impassively on the chair as her nose started to bleed. Walther spoke again,

"Susan, I want to have another look around upstairs, will you be all right down here alone with her?" He asked, nodding in Joan's direction.

"Yes I'll be fine." She replied as Walther moved towards her,

"I'll leave the gun with you just in case." He handed it over, Susan felt encouraged by the weight of it. Walther had been gone for only a few seconds when Joan spoke,

"May I go to the bathroom?" She had been wiping the blood from her nose using her sleeve, Susan assented,

"Don't lock the door, I'll wait outside." They crossed the hallway and Joan spoke again,

"Can I take my handbag? It's my time of the month and I'd-" Susan nodded before she finished her sentence and Joan picked up her handbag from a side table, then walked on to the downstairs bathroom, Joan leading with the gun in her back. They reached the little bathroom door, Joan went in and quickly closed it, then Susan heard the lock being turned, she shouted,

"Damn it I told you not to lock it! Open the door

now!" Then Susan heard little bleeping noises from the other side of the door, Joan was using her mobile phone from her bag. Susan lost her mind in sudden panic and banged on the door with the butt of the gun, it took her a few more seconds to think of shooting the lock off, then she pointed the barrel towards the handle and pulled the trigger. The intensity of the blast sent her back a pace and she let off more rounds almost randomly at the door. Within seconds Walther was by her side, taking the gun from her as the door drifted quietly open. Through the smoke they saw Joan's bloody corpse sprawled across the toilet

"She called someone, I'm sure I heard her whispering." Susan muttered, pointing to the phone still in her hand. Walther checked her pulse,

"Nothing. I think we had better leave. Did you touch anything?"

"No..." She replied blankly, "...Nothing." Walther took her by the arm, and after looking out of the front window led her to the car.

The house in the Countryside ~ 2000

Raven loved to be on horseback, to ride free and fast. Often before breakfast she would visit the stables, saddle up her favourite, Majesty, and lead her out into the fields.

"Fly Majesty, fly!" She whispered as she crossed the field at a full gallop. She had risen early and set off while the morning air was still cold, riding hard and fast until her muscles ached. With mixed feeling of elation and regret she turned her steed back to the stables at a gentler trot. Franco was waiting for her when she returned; she could see from his face that something was wrong,

81

"Joan telephoned." He called out to her as she approached,

"Why? What's happened?" She replied, sensing it was in no way good. Franco continued more quietly as she pulled up beside him,

"Her exact words were, before the gunfire started, *It's his wife and another man, they're here looking for him and they've got a gun!*" Raven climbed down slowly and handed the reins to him,

"You say you heard gunfire? Who was shooting? Joan or the others?"

"My guess, Mistress, is that Joan has been killed, I got the idea from the way she was speaking that she was trying to warn you."

"Was Sir Clive with her?"

"She did not say." They continued the conversation while they stabled the horse and walked back to the house. The stables were situated at the rear and to the side of the house, the gravelled path crunched under their feet. Raven paused at the doorstep and turned around to face away from the house. She looked at the lawns and the trees and beyond them the open fields, and she sighed gently before looking at Franco,

"We shall have to go back to Hammersmith, I need to know what's happened. Get ready, we will leave shortly. But first I think I'll have a chat with our guest Mr Richard Bryant."

A few minutes later she entered the attic room that served as a jail for Richard, the twins had removed his handcuff and replaced it with a chain around his ankle. They had also found him some clothes, he stood a few feet away from the bed and staring out of the small window. He knew she was there but didn't turn around, he wasn't going

82

to tell her anything more about Susan. Raven waited only a few seconds before demanding tersely,

"Has she got a gun?" Richard remained silent. Raven baited him,

"Perhaps you would you like me to bring her here, to be with you? Oh no, I'd better not do that, the twins wouldn't like it, they don't like sharing." Richard came unglued immediately and whirled around, jabbing his finger at Raven's face,

"You stay away from her!" He yelled, she smiled, unperturbed by his threatening manner, enjoying his discomfort,

"She's quite pretty isn't she?" Raven waved his wallet photo in the air, he made a move to grab it but she nimbly stepped backwards and stayed near to the door, still taunting him,

"I know someone who'd like to meet her. He likes pretty girls. Trouble is they're not very pretty when he's finished with them, if you know what I mean?"

Richard balled his fists and paced around his bed, but could not think of anything to say,

"Please, just leave her alone." He pleaded.

"Sorry. I can't. She's been poking her nose in where it does not belong..." Raven's tone implied that she had no choice, "...You see, she's been to the other house. And she took a man with her, who is he?" Richard groaned inside, he guessed that Susan and Walther had been looking for him,

"I don't know." He replied. Raven waited for a few moments before she spoke again, her voice suddenly turned to acid,

"You can have the photo, at least then you'll have something to remember her by!" She threw it to the floor and fled the room.

*

Cairo stood breathless in the gloom of a forgotten corridor after a game of it. She was sixteen, although she herself wasn't exactly sure how old she was, and her shabby clothes and uncultured manner made her appear more childlike. She whispered to herself,

"Cairo, you're a very silly girl!" A lifetime of near solitude left her talking to herself and inventing many imaginary friends,

"Yes but she's very brave too!" She heard one of them say. The hushed conversations continued as she wound her way through the warren of abandoned secret passages at the heart of the old house.

The house had been built around a central column of tiny staircases and passages designed by the master of the house so that he could move around without being seen by the servants. The passageways connected with all the landings of the main house and many of its rooms. The levers to the entrances to that secret domain were ingeniously concealed in the fine timber mouldings and architraves of the opulent old place. And although the current occupiers were aware of their existence they had fallen in to disuse many years before.

Cairo lay on her back in the dust and gloom. Hands at her side she wondered what it would be like to be a ghost.

Gradually her mind turned to the odd assortment of people in the house. There was Anjelica the housekeeper, who just about ran the house (armed with her lashing tongue and fueled by Sir Clive's fine brandy).

The Irish Cook, Fidelma, she was nice but had a wicked temper, and was always "Far too busy to stand around gossiping to silly young girls."

There was the gardener, Mr Underhill, he was a strange old man who never spoke. Cairo could remember being fascinated by his enormous calloused hands, she sometimes watched him as he worked, never speaking, just quietly sitting close by, pretending to be looking elsewhere.

Then there was Sir Clive; she had never had much to do with him. Most of the time he was away in London, wherever that was. She remembered that he gave her nice presents at Christmas but then there was that time she spied on him during the night in one of the upstairs bedrooms. There had been guests at the house staying over and one of them was a young woman not much older than herself. She'd thought it would be fun to visit her in the night but when she peeked through one of her spy-holes she could see that Sir Clive was there, he was 'doing things' to the girl that she obviously didn't like, she was crying but he wouldn't stop, he said it was too late to stop and that it was her fault for leading him on. Cairo stayed away from Sir Clive after that,

"Horrid fat man." all her friends agreed on that.

And then there was the chauffeur. Kelvin Bright by name, a slimy thin man who stunk of cigarettes and liked to swagger around carrying a large shotgun. Some years before he had brought five Rottweiler puppies to the house, at first they were lovely animals but his systematic training had turned them into vicious, aggressive guard dogs. She stayed away from him as well. She giggled as she remembered what Anjelica always called Kelvin behind his back,

"Greasy little ponce."

London, Hammersmith

Raven and Franco took the twins with them when they returned to the Hammersmith house in the early afternoon, It was a dry, blustery day with bright sunny intervals and occasional iron-grey clouds. They entered the house warily but it was soon apparent that apart from poor Joan's gory remains there was no one else inside.

Raven peered at the mess through the bathroom door and easily put two and two together,

"Shot her through the door while she was talking to you."

Franco looked closely at the bullet holes and Joan's wounds,

"It was an old gun by the looks of it, World War two probably."

"Doesn't matter now. But it was lucky that Sir Clive wasn't here"

"He must still be at the Club." Franco suggested.

"Yes, and he will probably not return until late this evening, we should clean up in here." She set the twins to work, cleaning up the blood and gore of their mother's body. They cried, quietly, wiping away the tears and snot with their cleaning rags. Franco took pity on them, he carried Joan's body and laid it on her bed. Raven offered a little condolence,

"Sir Clive will see to her funeral, I'm sure he will give her a good send-off." They nodded and dried their eyes, they never liked her anyway. With a look to each other they raised a question,

"When can we leave?"

"Richard will be getting hungry."

Raven shook her head in amazement and spoke to Franco,

"Take them back to the house. I will wait for Sir Clive..." She favoured him with a smile, "...Come and collect me tomorrow."

*

Sir Clive was mightily inconvenienced by Joan's death,

"Dash it all, now I shall have to find a new one..." He stood at her bedside, Raven beside him, "...What the devil happened to her anyway?"

"We think she must have surprised a burglar."

"Ah, I see." He swallowed the explanation and Raven planted a seed,

"Not the sort of thing you want to see in the newspaper is it?"

"Good lord no! That wouldn't do at all, dashed paparazzi all over the place!" Raven smiled,

"Poking their noses in and asking questions."

"Bloody intolerable!"

Sir Clive used his connections to have Joan's death certified as Natural Causes and arranged a quiet funeral in the local authority cemetery.

The twins would get to wear black dresses, and the whole inconvenient affair would vanish without a trace.

London, Windsor

Susan and Walther sat quietly in her living room. Since they had returned from the house in Hammersmith

Susan had been quietly going crazy. Walther watched her helplessly as she wandered from room to room, she tidied things and put laundry in the machine, she made coffee and sandwiches, but she refused to speak about the shooting or her husband. Finally, she broke down. Walther heard a small crash from the kitchen followed by some muffled whimpering, he quickly ran to the kitchen and found her kneeling on the floor with her head in her hands, the remains of a coffee cup were scattered on the floor in front of her, with a face contorted with grief she spat out the words,

"Richard's mug." She sobbed for several minutes before either of them spoke, eventually the spasm was over,

"What are we going to do?" she asked in a strengthening waver. Walther eased her onto a stool,

"My guess is that Raven has another safe house somewhere, we have to find it. Richard may be held captive there." He was reluctant to say what he really thought, that Richard was already dead. Susan seemed to think on his comment for a few moments then uttered,

"Is it true what they say about killing? That the second one is always easier?" Walther frowned and suggested she lie down for a while, he led her to the bottom of the stairs. She climbed them without another word.

The house in the Countryside - 2000

Richard had been exploring his cell, the iron bed was heavy but he could drag it backwards and forwards which meant that he could reach all four corners of the room. He tugged the plain wooden wardrobe away from the wall slightly and saw the outline of a tiny white painted door,

"How fucking creepy is that." He muttered to himself, then shook his head at the craziness of his situation. After carefully pushing the wardrobe back to its original position he dragged himself across the room and examined the bedroom door. It was locked and very solidly made. He turned away with a grunt, and was staring out of the window again when the twins returned chattering nonsense as usual,

"We're sorry we can't stay for very long, we had to go to London to-"

"-And now we've got to catch up with our chores." Richard noticed that they were wearing a lot of make-up and that their short dresses were not the kind of style you'd expect for doing 'chores'.

"I have to go to the toilet again!" He announced firmly. The infantile women looked at the buckets and then at him,

"Go ahead..." They announced, "...We're not shy." They giggled.

"Well I bloody well am!..." He retorted, "...I'm not shitting in front of an audience! I'm not a bloody animal. And I want a shave and a shower!" He was testing them to see how far he could go. At first they looked a little defiant, then crestfallen, then after their customary pause said,

"Shy? We hadn't thought of that." Without another word to each other, Emm stepped forward and handcuffed his right wrist to the top of the bed while Pip unlocked the ankle cuff from the bed and attached it to her own ankle, then they spoke,

"We will let you use the bathroom if you promise not to try to run away."

"You have to give us your word!" They waited until Richard duly promised,

89

"I swear on my cats' life." And Emm freed his wrist, whispering,

"He has a cat."

"That's nice." Pip then skipped lightly towards the door forgetting that she was shackled to Richard and fell over. There followed a strange little ritual where Emm helped Pip to get up asking her if she was all right and making a terrible fuss about nothing. Pip looked as if she was about to cry before Richard realised that he was also supposed to offer some kind of comfort to her,

"Would you like me to kiss it better?" He offered sarcastically. The effect was immediate; she lifted her leg and showed him a little red mark on her knee,

"Yes please..." She murmured in a forlorn voice, "...It hurts." Richard noticed that her legs had recently been shaven and the scent of perfume. He solemnly kissed her knee. When he looked up he saw Pip grinning at Emm with a triumphant look on her face, Emm did not look pleased at all.

"Is it all better now?" Richard asked, oozing false concern. Emm was the one who answered,

"Yes I think you are quite all right now, aren't you Philippa?" They exchanged glances with each other and led Richard out of the room.

"Shyness is nice." Pip declared with a broad smile.

A roadside camp, southern England

Tsuba stood in the trees out of sight of the lay-by. After a bow to the tree, he climbed it. Settled high in the boughs he looked beyond the trees to the town, from a pocket he removed a small notebook, after ruffling through for a moment he nodded and climbed back down the tree.

"I'll follow you and make a heaven out of hell, and I'll die by your hand which I love so well."

His face betrayed little emotion as he returned to the lay-by, collecting firewood on his way.

The house in the Countryside - 2000

The twins were peering around the bathroom door, their eyes more saucer-like than ever. Richard had stripped down to his boxers and finished using the toilet, but didn't have time to protest as they tiptoed in and locked the door. Emm carried a small safety razor and some shaving cream; Pip had a small bundle of clothes that she placed on a small cupboard behind the door. There was a small stool in a corner, Emm placed it in front of the basin, draped a towel over it and sat Richard down,

"Shave first? Or hair wash?" She asked, her face flushed with excitement.

"I don't need any help shaving, I'm a big boy now and have been doing it myself-" The girls silenced him by each placing a finger on his lips, explaining,

"You're not allowed to have anything sharp. The Mistress would kill us, or worse..." They shuddered, "...She says you might turn it into a weapon to kill us and escape..." They nodded to each other, "...And so we've decided to wash your hair first, then shave you..." Emm licked her lips, "...And finish you off with a good scrubbing." They giggled, adding a little apologetically,

"You have become a little smelly." Despite feeling very silly at first Richard went along with the surreal operation; it felt weird-good to be pampered even if it was

91

by a pair of lunatics.

"Quite handsome, don't you think Pip?" Emm had finished shaving Richard's beard off and they both paused to study his bruised and swollen face.

"Now stand up, let's get you washed." Emm's voice had taken on a husky tone as he stood up between the girls, Richard was also starting to feel a little uncomfortable,

"Hold on, this isn't nec-" Without warning Emm yanked his boxers down,

"Hey!..." He quickly yanked them back up, "...What the-"

"He's being shy again."

"Silly isn't he?" Richard took them by the shoulders and turned them around,

"Just get out of here, I'll do the rest myself!" After a short pause the twins scooped up the shaving things as one and left the bathroom,

"Call us when you've finished." Their voices cold.

*

Cairo's bedroom was a grubby shambles. Once upon a time it had been decorated for a child, possibly fifty years earlier that child had grown up and left. And the room had never been touched since. She had lots of shelf space, two chests, a cupboard and a wardrobe. And the floor. It looked as if a giant had picked up the room and shaken it so that everything had fallen over or tilted on the skew, or on to the floor itself.

From the window-seat she gazed for a while at the dusty, cobweb-strewn mobiles hanging from the ceiling, Victorian glass fairies danced in the late afternoon sunlight. With a gentle sigh she stood up and skittered

92

across the room, effortlessly avoiding the randomly strewn toys, books and other abandoned artefacts. She reached the secret door neatly concealed within the panelling below the dado rail. She pressed the hidden lever and had to stoop slightly to enter the dark passage beyond.

London, The Gas Lamp Inn

In the bar of The Gas Lamp Inn, Raven forced a smile as the man they had arranged to meet lumbered across to join them. Franco wouldn't even try to be polite to the big man, he detested him and suffered his company only because of his loyalty to Raven.

Smokey Dick pulled up a chair with a curt nod to Franco and threw himself down onto it, growling in a thick phlegmy voice,

"Long time no see, princess!" He always referred to Raven as princess. Franco slitted his eyes and clenched his fists. Raven replied in a friendly but business-like tone,

"Yes Dick, a long time, but let's not waste any more time with any idle chat, I have a job for you. There's a woman I want you to, er, see to." Raven had hooked him instantly at the mention of 'woman' and 'see to'. Franco could see his depraved mind working, he watched as Dick's mouth watered while he rubbed his greasy palms together.

"How old?" Dick asked.

"Young. And pretty." Raven replied. Franco felt a wave of pity for Susan. Dick let smoke waft out his mouth as he spoke,

"When?" He asked.

"Now." She stated simply. There was a pause while Dick drank and blew out more smoke. Franco promised himself that one day he would snuff-out Smokey Dick.

Dick coughed and cleared his throat before asking,

"Is 'e coming?" He demanded wagging a thick smoke-stained finger at Franco. Franco responded before Raven,

"Yes. I will drive, I do not think I will be needed to administer the punishment." Franco stared dagger-eyed at Dick while he spoke. Raven felt the tension between the two men, it was like a physical thing to her and it felt so good. The excitement and hunger was growing within her more and more as the minutes passed, a frenzy was coming on and she craved for satisfaction, the kind of satisfaction she only knew one way to achieve.

London, Windsor

Walther sat in an armchair in the living room, it was dark outside and the house was quiet, he hoped that Susan would sleep for a while, he wanted time to think. He gazed absently around the room and noticed that the answer phone had a message waiting to be played, although strictly-speaking, he had no right to do it, he reasoned that it might be an important message and should be heard as soon as possible. He toyed with the idea of calling Susan down to hear it but in the end he decided to leave her in bed, it turned out to be a message from Cyndy asking about her wages and if she should bother to turn up for work on Monday morning as there was no office left?

Walther fell back into the armchair to continue his deliberations on their next move.

He drifted into a light sleep and was startled awake by the front door bell. He rose stiffly from the chair and made his way to the door, Susan was at the top of the stairs in her dressing gown and called down to him to put the security chain on before opening the door. It was too late, as soon as Walther had turned the latch the door burst inwards catching him above his left eye, blood poured into it immediately blinding him, he never saw the set of brass knuckles coming towards him on the bulging fist of Smokey Dick, Susan squealed in horror as Dick smashed Walther's face, he was down and out but Dick didn't stop, he pummelled on Walther's chest and stomach until he lay still. Susan ran down the stairs screaming at Dick,

"Get off him you bastard! Leave him alone!" Dick lashed out a swift backhand and knocked her flying into the wall, he stood up and waved his bloodied metal-stud fist in front of her face, behind him Raven had come in quietly and closed the door,

"Check the rest of the house!" She ordered as she reached between her legs for the slim dagger and held it at Susan's throat,

"Any trouble from you and I'll cut out your tongue! And then I'll give you to him to play with!" She laughed as she waved towards Dick. Susan was too terrified to speak.

"No one else here!" Dick called down from the top of the stairs, roughly the same spot that Susan had been in. Raven led them into the living room where she tied Susan's hands behind her back, Smokey Dick stood in front of her, he was breathing hard and his lips were wet, his hands were shaking, suddenly he reached out and tore the front of her dressing gown apart, he started crudely groping over her body with his hard coarse hands. Mumbling and dribbling he rubbed the front of his jeans. Susan fell backwards as Raven yanked her by the hair, she was bundled onto the dining table as Dick spread her legs.

"Hold her steady!..." Raven commanded as she held the knife to Susan's face, "...Something to remember us by..."

she purred as she slid the point into the soft flesh of Susan's cheek,

"Ess..." She worked the tip with swift precision,

"Ell..." Susan's terror cranking her lust,

"Yew..." she finished the last letter with a shiver of pleasure,

"Tee..." and leaned back to admire her handiwork, "... Here, take a look!" She produced a small make up mirror and held it in front of Susan's face, through the blood she could make out the word SLUT carved across her left cheek. The sight of her ravaged face triggered Susan into a terrified frenzy, she kicked at Dick and bucked up and down to try to get free, it was no use, Dick was a very strong man and the more she struggled the more he liked it. He pulled her closer to him and prepared to enter her, Susan spat and swore and cried all at once, she felt his hardness against her, and closed her eyes in anguish.

And then all three of them heard the doorbell. They froze for a second and at long last Susan found her scream, she screamed for her life until Raven punched her in the face,

"Quiet or I'll slit your throat." Dick hurriedly yanked up his jeans and headed for the door. They heard a girl's voice calling through the letterbox,

"Richard! Susan! are you in there? Oh my god!" It was Cyndy at the door and as she peered through the letterbox she saw Walther's smashed face and then Dick making straight for the door, she stepped back and reached quickly into her handbag and set off a personal attack alarm, the door flew open and Dick made a grab for her, Cyndy was too quick for him and pepper-sprayed him in the face, followed instantly by a powerful kick to the groin. Dick bellowed,

96

"Fucking bitch!" And fell backwards into the house. Susan rolled off the table and quickly managed to get to her feet expecting another attack. Raven had vanished, Susan looked quickly around the room and then heard Cyndy shouting for help outside, with her hands still tied behind her back she gingerly made her way into the hall, she saw Dick stagger backwards before righting himself and racing out of the house at a shambling run. Cyndy was shouting for help and banging on all the neighbours doors, then when she saw Susan she gasped, stopped shouting and ran inside to her with her arms outstretched,

"Oh my god, oh my god! What's he done to you!?" Cyndy burst into a flood of hysterical tears as she wrapped the dressing gown back around Susan. They stood pressed against each other for a moment, unable to speak, then Susan saw Walther,

"We must call an ambulance!" Cyndy struggled to untie Susan's hands,

"Hurry!"

"I am!..." Cyndy shook the ropes free, "...And the police!"

The neighbours had started gathering outside, one of them, a casual friend, came into the house to help. Dick had run off, Raven had vanished, Susan passed out.

The house in the Countryside - 1999

Cairo's feline nocturnal wanderings had always been restricted to the confines of the house, it was at the height of the previous summer that she discovered a way out into the eerily beautiful garden.

Late one evening she had stood out on the balcony of one of the sealed upstairs rooms, staring at the stars and listening to the many small noises coming up from the garden and nearby woods. A small movement noticed from the corner of her eye made her turn and look down. A tiny field mouse scampered along the balcony rail and jumped off into the dark. Cairo's curiosity was aroused and she peered over the rail, she realised for the first time that the large tree that grew close to the house had stretched a thick bough that brushed the wall just below the balcony. She looked for the mouse but it had gone, with only the slightest hesitation Cairo climbed up over the balcony and put her weight on the bough, still holding on to the rail she jumped up and down to test its strength, it was solid. She thought for a while about trying to climb down to the ground but could see that the branches and twigs were too densely interwoven for her to get through. Undeterred she climbed back onto the balcony and scampered into her warren of secret passages. Her destination was the kitchen, once there she borrowed the key to Anjelica's store cupboard which was located at the end of a bleak corridor at the back of the house. The cupboard was in reality a small room, rammed with every kind of never-to-be-thrown-away 'useful thing' you could ever think of. She found a small saw and a few yards of rope, and then couldn't resist pulling open the drawers of a huge cupboard. In the second drawer down she saw a penknife, she grabbed it immediately, drawn to the carved mother-of-pearl handle,

"Beautiful." She murmured, opening the blade and admiring the shining steel. With a half-smile she popped it into her pocket, ran out and locked the door, returned the key to the kitchen and breathlessly scurried back to the balcony and the tree. With the rope tied around her waist she hopped over the rail onto the bough. Then, using the

98

saw, she carefully cut a passage just large enough for her to pass through the dense branches. It was hard work at first, trying to stay balanced and use the saw at the same time, but her work became easier as she approached the lower levels of the branches.

It was nearly dawn when she at last touched the trunk of the tree at about six feet above ground.

She had worked all through the short summer night, her hair had been pulled and her face scratched by the hundreds of little branches, her fingers were sore and dirty, and yet she felt elated. Ignoring her tiredness she uncoiled the rope and wrapped it around the branch she was sitting on, without pausing to test it she dropped off the branch and slid down the rope, she was too tired to hang on and fell most of the way to the ground burning her palms on the coarse rope, her feet touched ground first, closely followed by her bottom, for a few seconds she lay on the grass on her back staring upwards at the tree. Then slowly she pulled herself upright to examine the world outside the house.

London, Windsor

Franco saw the look of displeasure on Raven's face as he opened the car door for her, knowing her moods he kept silent. She sat in the back seat and pursed her lips in thought before speaking,

"We will wait a few moments for the oaf." Franco sensed that she had run out of patience with Dick, then they both saw him running around the corner towards them, he wrenched open the car door and threw himself into the seat next to Raven, he was panting and out of breath but still managed to shout,

"Don't just fuckin' sit there! Let's get the fuck out of

here!" Franco waited expressionlessly until Raven gave the order to drive, Dick continued to rant,

"Fuckin' little bitch got me right in the fuckin' bollocks!" He sat in the car seat with his legs wide apart pressing against Raven, she squeezed herself forward and whispered to Franco for a few moments.

"Whatcha fuckin' whisperin' about!? Ain't I good enough to talk to no more!?" He yelled angrily. They ignored him. Franco drove for a couple of minutes and then turned the car off the main road and into a run-down area of boarded-up shops and slums.

Dick was mumbling and moaning, and with an unexpected lunge, he grabbed Raven's hand and guided it towards his groin,

"Here Princess, rub this better for me~!" He did not get chance to finish his sentence, Franco braked sharply and was out of the car in a second, he reached in and yanked the big man out of the back seat with ease. Dick threw a punch that Franco effortlessly blocked before stepping forward and grabbing Dick's head between his big powerful hands. There was a dreadful clicking sound as with a sudden irresistible twist he broke Dick's fat neck. Dick felt the sudden pain and even he was not stupid enough to not realise that his neck was useless. The two men made eye contact while Franco held Dick's head upright balanced on the end of his forefinger.
Franco spoke quietly,

"If I move my finger your head will fall forward and you will die." Dick didn't move a muscle, he was too scared to speak or move.

"Raise your arms!" Franco ordered. Slowly and painfully Dick raised his arms and held on to his own head. Franco pulled his finger away and stepped back while

Dick stood in the middle of the road swaying and holding his head upright.

The men heard soft laughter, it was Raven, she had found the scene quite amusing,

"Oh Franco, you do know how to cheer a girl up!" She laughed. Franco got back in the car and they drove off leaving Dick still holding his head and standing in the middle of the road. Eventually he plucked up the courage to try to walk, plodding like Frankenstein's monster he moved gingerly forward. Unable to turn to see, he heard a car turn into the street, it was going fast and sounded its horn as it approached,

"Get da fuck outta da way man!" A voice snarled at him as the car missed him by an inch. Dick's heart sank as he heard the screech of brakes and through the corner of an eye he saw the car turn back towards him, dizzy and sobbing he tried to stagger away.

"What da fuck you dooin' man?" The voice called out from the car as it slowly drove by then turned again to stop in front of him. Two men stepped out and stood in front of him,

"Whatchoo holding yo head for man?" It didn't seem like a friendly inquiry,

"Let's see what you got in them pockets." One of the men reached forward, Dick's reflexes got the better of him and he let go of his head, it was a fatal mistake. The two men jumped back in shock as Dick's head flopped aimlessly forward.

"Whoaa!" One of them yelled as they stepped back. Dick tried to speak, to beg for help as he stared at his own gut, but no sound would come except for a thin gurgle, he flailed about for a second or two trying to regain control but the blood circulation to his brain was cut off and he

101

quickly fell to the ground. His world went dark as he lost consciousness, he was dead a few moments later.

The two men gaped in amazement for a few seconds, then took the opportunity to empty his pockets and drive off. Neither of them having noticed the old lady watching them from the shelter of the little park opposite, with Hugo's fresh dog-poo still warm in her hand.

Raven, on the prowl ~ London

Franco drove Raven deeper into central London, she was still angry and frustrated about Susan's escape from full punishment, she needed more satisfaction and the night was still young. They ended up at a nightclub in Soho, once inside they split up, Raven pretended to be alone while Franco watched from a distance, she flirted with several different men until she found the type she wanted, then she threw out her hook and reeled him in. He was Asian, early thirties, making lots of ready cash through restaurants and drugs, he was married but also rented an apartment for 'business purposes' and he was used to getting what he wanted. She made it obvious that she was available and by the early hours of the morning they were cruising through the city towards his apartment.

"Stop the car!" She suddenly demanded. They were passing through a red light district where there were dozens of girls on the street.

"Stop? What for, baby?" The man was puzzled.

"Pick one!..." She said pointing at the prostitutes and smiling, "...Let's have a real party!" The man looked at her for a few seconds, weighing her up, he decided that she was a spoilt rich bird 'roughing it' for kicks, he would open her eyes tonight. He drove the BMW slowly forward, casting his lust filled eyes over the girls on offer, he chose one.

"Her!" He pointed to a small white girl, very young looking with bleached blonde hair, she looked little more than a child. Raven got out of the car and sauntered over to her, a few moments later they were both in the back of the car giggling while the man drove them to his apartment. Franco watched and followed discreetly.

The apartment was a little disappointing; above a row of shops and consisting of a small office in the front room, a combined bathroom and toilet, a small kitchen area and a bed-sitting room, it was seedy but would nevertheless still suit Raven's purpose. The man got the atmosphere going with some music and a couple of bottles of sparkling wine, after a few minutes he started on the young whore, he tore off her clothes and roughly manhandled her. Raven stripped them both and encouraged them, savouring their mixed emotions. She could tell that the man preferred violent sex and made no effort to discourage it, as the minutes passed he became increasingly violent and abusive, the mixed waves of passion emanating from the pair of them became a heady cocktail for Raven to enjoy.
She was still half dressed when he called out to her,

"C'mon baby, get that kit off, don't you wanna join in?" He motioned for her to join the girl kneeling in front of him. Raven smiled and slipped out of her remaining clothes, her knife comfortably concealed in her left palm. She had enjoyed the waves of pain and hate coming from them both but it was now time for the next level. She knelt in front of him, her face next to the girl's, and smiled up at him as he slapped her face,

"C'mon y'fuckin'bitches." Her smile never wavered as she took him in hand. And then with a purr the knife was

103

next to his penis, his eyes widened in terror as with a powerful stroke she lopped it off.

Events seemed then to move with exaggerated slowness, blood poured from between his legs, the young whore recoiling in horror. The look of surprise on the man's face did not reflect the terror and pain he felt as he saw his manhood in Raven's right hand. She remained in a kneeling position, she could not stand; the waves coming from his mind were so intense she was left temporarily paralysed. She had found out long before that nothing affected a man quite as completely as emasculation.

The man staggered backwards, his hands shaking at his sides as he stared down at himself, Raven slowly rose up in front of him, she seemed taller, her face aglow, she was only seconds away from complete ecstasy, with a nimble step forward she curled her right leg behind his and pushed forwards, he fell backwards, she straddled him and plunged down the dagger, she felt it grate exquisitely as it passed between his ribs, her moment of ecstasy had come at last, she bucked and writhed against him, shuddering through spasms of pleasure as his life drained out of him.

When it was over she felt rejuvenated, strong and more full of life than ever before, it felt as if she had absorbed his life force into her own, and it felt clean and pure.

The young whore sat huddled tightly into a corner, silently sobbing. She had been on the streets for a few months but nothing she had experienced had prepared her for this. Raven crossed the room towards her, her voice low and calming,

"Feel no pity for him, he had it coming. Don't be afraid, I will not harm you." She lied. The girl looked up, Raven looked regal, naked blood-spattered, she took the

104

girl's hand, made her stand, then led her across to the man's body, with a movement that was almost sleight-of-hand Raven slit the girl's left wrist. The girl moaned and whimpered as she watched her own blood pouring out over the dead man's body, She whimpered,

"Please, no." Raven held her tightly until the girl collapsed, then with terrifying efficiency she set about obliterating any evidence of her own presence in the flat. She went to the kitchen and found a knife of comparable size to her own dagger, pressed it into the palms of both of the girl's hands several times and forced it into the hole in the dead man's chest making it appear to be the murder weapon, then she placed the man's lopped-off penis into the girl's hand and stood back to survey the scene.

When she was satisfied, she washed, dressed and quietly left. Franco waited as ever in the car at about a hundred yards away, it was almost dawn.

*

Raven dozed wile they drove through the quiet early light.

Franco could see her in the rear-view mirror, and a memory surfaced. He recalled the time they'd first met. It was 1937, he was a child in the blazing ruins of Guernica. He had followed her through the streets for days without her noticing him, it was one of those curious twists of fate that seem improbable and yet always seem to occur at precisely the right, or wrong, moment. The small military unit that she was with had been caught by a surprise attack, half of the men were wiped out instantly by grenades and Raven was thrown to the ground as her horse was shot, she was caught between the two lines of fire and

105

certain to be killed, Franco ran, heedless of the bullets to save her, he took her hand and led her down the narrow rubble-strewn lanes of the old city to safety.

He could no longer remember how they ended up staying together, but he would never forget the first time she looked into his eyes, she seemed to see straight into his mind and soul, he was shocked at first and looked away, then he looked back into her eyes and surrendered himself, he would be hers to command for eternity.

London, Windsor

Susan stared into the bathroom mirror, she was at home after discharging herself from the hospital in the morning following the attack. She had visited Walther briefly, he had been asleep and a nurse described his condition as 'stable'. She went home alone and stood in the hallway with the memories of the previous few days events crowding her mind.

"The scars will fade eventually." They had said at the hospital. Susan continued to stare into the mirror. Her left cheek was covered with a large soft bandage but she could all too easily picture the damage beneath it. From the base of her right cheek a thin dark line crossed her face in a diagonal line across the bridge of her nose and ending on the left side of her forehead. Carefully she lifted the bandage from her cheek exposing Raven's cruel handiwork, the skin was swollen and bruised but could do nothing to hide the letters carved out so very neatly. A single tear like a raindrop fell down Susan's ravaged face, before the sight of it sent her into a rage, she banged her fist against the mirror,

"I'm not going to cry! You won't make me cry!" She

106

shouted at her reflection and punched again at the mirror, never had she felt so alone and so frightened. And so very, very, wronged. There was a feeling of emptiness in her soul, everything that she loved had been taken away from her, Richard, her parents, her entire life! The emptiness left a gap that needed to be filled, so she filled it, with hate and rage she filled the gap in her heart.

So Susan packed a suitcase, there was nothing left to stay for. Without leaving a note or phoning anyone she left her home for good. Carefully and methodically she packed only the things that really mattered to her, then she went to the bank and withdrew all the cash that she could before starting the long drive to her parent's cottage in Norfolk. She was going 'home', for the first time in ten years, not for sanctuary but for information, she hoped that somewhere in her parents careful research of the woman they knew as Raven she might find a clue, a lead, or just some idea about what to do next.

The house in the Countryside ~ 2000

Wide awake in the middle of the night Richard lay on his bed and watched the shadows cast by the moonlight. The tree outside swayed to and fro making them dance around his cell-like room. It was cold so he wrapped himself in all the clothes available to him. A small sound from the corner of the room gave him a start and he rose to investigate, as he stood he heard a sudden intake of breath, turning quickly he saw a pale face disappear behind the wardrobe,

"Hey! Who's there?" He dragged his bed across to the wardrobe and heaved it away from the wall, the little door was open by an inch, *"Looked like a child."* he waited for a few moments then spoke softly,

"Don't be shy, come out and say hello. I don't bite." He said it as conversationally as possible under the circumstances. The face reappeared, slowly followed by slim shoulders and the rest of the body. Cairo stood with her feet together and her hands clasped in front of her, framed in the moonlight she was a pale and ghostly vision. Her white nightdress glowed luminous and angelic, tight around the neck and reaching down to her knees. But despite her air of youth and innocence Richard could see the family likeness instantly, he had no doubt that the little girl before him was Raven's daughter. She spoke, her voice solemn and measured,

"I've been watching you." She stared into his eyes,

"I don't think I like being spied on." Richard replied whilst wondering if she had seen him with the idiot flirtatious twins.

"It's not spying...!" She retorted indignantly, "...I watch everyone. I know everything that goes on in this house!" She spoke like a child caught being naughty. There was a few moments silence while Richard thought of what to say, wondering if he could use her to his advantage,

"Does your mother know where you are?" He asked.

"My mother? No. Why would she?" The question seemed to confuse her. Richard , sensed an opportunity,

"Can you help me escape?" He rattled his chain for effect.

"Escape? Why? Aren't you happy here?" She stared down at his chain, the concept of being a prisoner had never occurred to her, she felt a kind of affinity with the idea.

"Where would you go?" She asked in total innocence. Her naiveté amazed Richard, he formed the

108

impression that she did not know much about the outside world. He looked at her tiny teenage frame, her small face with the large eyes,

"Have you ever been out of this house?" He asked intuitively.

"Yes of course I have. lots of times." Richard didn't believe her but at the same time he did not want to upset her by saying so, there was more to be gained by playing along with her,

"Well anyway, I'm pleased to meet you. My name is Richard." He held out his hand as if for a handshake, she smiled as if she didn't do it very often and curtsied, ignoring his outstretched hand. Richard realised that he was going to have to lead the conversation,

"So where do you go when you go out? Are there any shops near here?" Cairo's eyes darted towards the ceiling as she struggled to think of a convincing lie,

"I sometimes go to..." Her gaze remained firmly at the ceiling, "...The cinema!"

Richard grinned and stifled a snort, instantly regretting it as her face dropped and she retorted,

"Well it's none of your business anyway!" And in a flash she had disappeared behind the wardrobe, he heard the faint sound of the wooden door clunking shut. Richard fell backwards onto his bed, he was disappointed that he'd upset the girl so easily, it was good to know there were other people in the house. And that there was another way out of his cell. He mulled on it, working on the idea that Cairo might somehow be useful as a means of escape.

*

The gardener, Mr Underhill, was old but still strong,

109

his wife had died of cancer many years before and he'd never thought to find someone else. Their marriage had been childless and he'd resigned himself to serving the garden for the rest of his years. At five minutes to midnight he stood waiting under the dark overhanging branches of an ancient Willow tree waiting, hoping, for another glimpse of his Midnight Orchid. It was last summer when he first suspected that it might be about to bloom, he had found a scattering of cut twigs and leaves under the big old tree that grew close to the house. Curious as to their origin he climbed up into the tree to see from where they had been cut, at first he was puzzled, and he sat in the tree for a while until the answer came to him. He smiled to himself. Since then he regularly hid in the garden hoping she would appear. This night was cold and clear, lit by a bright half moon, he took up his hiding place under the curtain of Willow branches and waited, it was nearly an hour before Cairo appeared on the window balcony above the tree, she was wearing her white sleeping gown and had tied back her long dark hair with blue ribbons. She floated on the balcony in the midnight breeze. Mr Underhill sighed softly and whispered to himself,

"Ah, as lovely as a Midnight Orchid." He watched her climb gracefully down into the tree and drop to earth like a faery princess.

He watched her as she danced around the garden, she was as delightful as the flowers he nurtured so carefully all year round. She scampered here and there, sometimes out of sight, sometimes going very close to where Mr Underhill was hidden.

"Don't step on the shadows!" She called softly to one or all of her imaginary friends. He had watched her on so many nights she had danced her way into Mr Underhill's heart, he fell in love with her, as he loved the garden, she was a rare and beautiful addition to his garden that although he could not water or prune her he would watch over her, day and night, to make sure that she grew strong and healthy. Quietly, to himself, he pledged his life to her, his very own Midnight Orchid.

Cairo danced and played until dawn, shaking off the dust of a day spent dashing through the corridors. Mr Underhill watched with sadness as she climbed wearily back into the tree, his own fingers clenched tight as she gripped the rope to pull herself up, he wanted to run out to her and lift her to safety but he knew that he shouldn't. When she was gone he made his way back to his shack near the woods, he lay down to rest.

In the moments before sleep he heard dogs barking.

London, Hospital

Walther was awake in hospital. A nurse and a doctor turned at his muffled grunting,

"I think he's trying to say something!" The muffled sounds coming through Walther's bandages could not be understood by either of them.

"Don't try to talk!" The man spoke slowly and clearly trying to make sure that Walther could understand him.

"Your face is heavily bandaged, we've had to perform some delicate reconstruction work on your jaw and cheek bones, so please don't try to speak just yet. You are in hospital and you're going to be all right!" The man flashed Walther his best reassuring smile and stepped backwards out of eyesight. Walther collapsed inwardly, he could tell that it was hopeless trying to communicate at that moment, he would have to wait to find out if Susan was okay. Gradually he drifted back to sleep.

Norfolk, England

After three hours of driving Susan turned off the main Norwich-to-Fakenham road into a narrow country lane. She was in the ancient unchanged countryside of Norfolk, the lane sloped gently downhill between farmland and woods towards a river, she recognised the old mill on her right as she passed over the single span stone bridge and knew that just around the bend she would see the village church. The sun was shining and there was a touch of Spring in the air, the village green was aglow with Daffodils, she was amazed that everything in the village looked pretty much the same as the last time she had seen it, ten years earlier.

Her parents' cottage, the house that she was born in and had called home until she left for university, was down an unsurfaced track that ran past the side of the village Pub and ended by the churchyard wall. She parked on the shingled area in the front garden, feeling nervous about seeing the old cottage again, ghosts of her parent's untimely deaths haunted her dreams and she'd spent years trying to block out the memories.

She stepped out of her car and immediately felt that something wasn't right about the place, but it took several moments for her to realise what it was, the house looked too neat and tidy. She had been expecting to find an old ruin with weeds and mile-high grass for a front garden, instead she saw that the front lawn had recently been mown and the rendered walls of the cottage had been painted, the thatching was all intact, it looked as if the house was lived in. She was confused, as far as she knew no one had rented

112

the house and she had not paid anyone to maintain it. With a small suitcase in her left hand she walked slowly to the front door catching a reflection of her bandaged cheek in a window as she dug into her handbag for the keys. Without warning a loud voice called out from behind her,

"I say! Can I help you? There's no one in the house at the moment!"

Susan felt hot and bothered, she had no desire to meet people in her present condition, but she recognised the voice and knew there would be no escape,

"Hello Vicar." She replied simply as she turned. He stared at her for a moment, then a flash of recognition passed across his face,

"It is you! My goodness how delightful! After all this time! How lovely to see you. Have you come back to stay?" As he approached he put his arms out to Susan who responded by forcing a smile. He looked closely at her bandaged face until she became even more uncomfortable. She replied in a cool dispassionate voice,

"No, I'm just visiting." She really wished he would go the hell away.

"Oh that is a pity! It would be so nice if the old cottage was lived in again!" Susan had found the front door key and wanted to go inside to get away from him, not because she disliked the kindly old man but because she was ashamed and embarrassed about her face and her reason for being there. And then she was dismayed when he reached out and took the key from her fingers,

"Let me open the door for you!" She remembered that he always had spoken too loudly, with an inward sigh she let him open the door and follow her inside. The junk-mail was piled neatly on the hall table with another larger pile underneath, next to that was a large cardboard box full of what looked like things to go to a car-boot sale. She was confused and had to ask,

"Vicar, what's going on? Someone's been coming into the house and cleaning up, and who's been doing the gardening?" The Vicar looked slightly embarrassed,

"Well my dear, I do hope you don't mind, it was me. I've been looking in on the old place from time to time, it seemed such a shame to let it fall into rack and ruin, and I've always hoped, in fact all of us hoped, that some day you would coming back." Susan did not like the sound of 'all of us', *"Perhaps it was a mistake to come back."* she thought but said nothing and walked into the living room. Vicar followed closely, still chattering,

"And as for the garden, that's been looked after by young Tommy Paston, you remember Tommy don't you?" She certainly did remember him, they had been close friends at school, almost inseparable, she hadn't seen him since she left for University, she was slightly surprised that he had stayed in the village remembering that he wanted to be a rock singer.

"He'll be thrilled to see you again!" The Vicar added. She whirled on him instantly,

"No! Don't tell him I'm here! I don't want to see anyone!" Susan spat out the words harshly, taking the Vicar by surprise. He again looked at her closely before gently asking,

"Don't you really mean that you don't want anyone to see **you**?..." He pointed at her face, "...Something terrible has happened and you've come home to hide from it." Susan glared at him. She hated him being right, she **did** want to hide from people.

"I just want to be alone for a while. That's all." She had to try hard to keep down her rising anger, *"Why won't he just take the hint and piss off!*" They'd drifted into the kitchen and the vicar went straight to the kettle,

"A cup of tea is what you need my dear, allow me to be mother."

Susan excused herself and went to the bathroom, by the time she returned he was pouring into two cups,

"There you are, come and sit down, you must be tired from your journey. This will be a nice little pick-me-up." She obediently sat at the kitchen table opposite him, hiding her shaking hands in her lap. He smiled, and with as much gentleness as he could muster asked,

"Have you been in a, erm, accident? A car perhaps?" His eyebrows shot up in surprise when Susan laughed loudly and bitterly, looked him in the eyes and ripped the bandage from her cheek. Rising to her feet she shouted,

"Ever seen a crash do this to someone's face!" She leaned forward across the table, turning her ruined cheek towards him, almost threateningly. The Vicar turned white, unable to speak, he was genuinely horrified. She ranted at him,

"Can you read it all right! Do you want to put your glasses on to get a better look!? Are you satisfied now?!" Susan vented her anger on him, unfairly she knew, but she didn't care, he shouldn't have been so nosey, she thought to herself. She watched as he tremblingly picked up his tea.

"Who needs a pick-me-up now?" She thought cruelly.

Chapter 4
"Your death is my life."

The house in the Countryside - 2000

Raven stared out of an open window, but of course not for very long, She was preparing herself to speak to Richard again and for some reason her mind had thrown up an ancient memory. Of Julius, and any reminders of that ill-fated liaison filled her with immediate revulsion. She pictured the last time she'd seen him, how he was so proud that he'd owned her. She shook her head as she had done more than a thousand times to remove his face and memory,

"Cute curly-haired monster." She hissed. He'd been such a bastard to her.

*

Cairo lay under her bed holding Button tightly in her arms,

"His name is Richard..." She whispered in its ear, "... He was a little bit horrid to me, but I think he quite likes me really. He's a prisoner you know!" She had been mulling over the idea of being held captive and found it very confusing but also quite exciting.

"Is he happy?" Button asked her. She gave it a little thought,

"Why shouldn't he be?" She asked. And then Button reminded her of something that happened when she was younger,

"Do you remember the time when you were in one of

the upstairs rooms and a little bird flew in through an open window?" Cairo remembered it all too vividly, even though she had tried to put it out of her mind, she nodded her head in the cramped confine underneath her bed. Button continued,

"You closed the window to keep it in, and the poor little thing went mad, it flew all around the room before crashing into the window pane, and then it died." Cairo remembered the incident all too well, she pictured the little bird dead on the carpet, a small drop of blood on the end of its tiny beak, she remembered sobbing uncontrollably with guilt and shame,

"I only wanted to be its friend!..." She felt stinging tears fill her eyes once again, "...I never meant to hurt it!" She wiped away the hot flood on her cheek with the back of a grubby hand.

Button said nothing.

Cairo made a decision.

*

Richard was sat on the edge of his iron bed while Raven lounged in the doorway, well out of his reach, his voice bitter,

"How can you sleep at night? Knowing what you've done to people?" He asked her. He had wanted to ask about Susan but felt too frightened of the answer he might receive.

"My conscience is none of your concern..." She replied in her light, airy fashion, "...Besides, I don't remember things for very long, I don't know why, but every so often memories just seem to fall out of my head. I can feel it, I know when it's happening but I can't control it. It's not

118

painful or anything, except I get a peculiar feeling afterwards, as if I'm missing something..." She laughed, and then continued, "...Who cares about a few dead people anyway? People die all the time. That's what I hate most about this 'modern' age, you're all so hypocritical! Who really gives a damn if someone on the other side of town gets killed? Who's going to remember in five minutes time anyway? I've ended a few miserable peoples' pathetic, shallow lives. So what? They deserved it anyway, most of them. I've done the world a good turn by getting rid of the scum, more air for the rest of us." She laughed heartily as she spoke. Richard shook his head, he wasn't sure if she actually meant any of what she'd said but she'd annoyed him again, he'd thought of Philip,

"My friend wasn't scum, he was a good man, he~" Raven cut him off,

"Ha! He was a nobody, a dribbling half-man. You should have seen the way he lusted after me. And he died sobbing!" Raven lied to Richard for the pleasure of feeling him suffer, she knew how to hurt in more ways than one, she stuck the knife into Richard's mind and then she twisted it some more,

"And as for that bitch wife of yours! Don't expect to see her 'pretty' little face again!" Richard clenched his fists and 'switched off', it was his only weapon against her until he could get free. He promised himself that one day he would get revenge. Raven did not like to be ignored and she always liked to have the last word,

"It's an interesting little trick, being able to switch off your mind like that, you've set a challenge for me, will I be able to break you? We shall have to see!"

She flounced petulantly out of his cell almost bumping into the twins as they arrived with his evening meal. They stopped dead in their tracks looking guiltily at the floor. Raven eyed them with suspicion which changed to amusement as she noted their heavily made-up faces and short dresses. She guessed immediately what was going on their minds, *"Mental little tarts..."* and wondered if Richard had been playing along with them, *"...He's probably got some sort of loyalty hang-up."* She laughed and called out over her shoulder as she turned the corner,

"Enjoy him while you can!" She breezed along the corridor, they heard her laughter continue all the way down the stairs. After a while of standing motionless in the corridor they joined Richard in his cell. They didn't hear him groan under his breath,

"Oh god, here they come again..." he faked a charming smile, "...Bonkers & Barmy inc."

*

Outside in the grounds of the house, the chauffeur, Kelvin Bright by name, was 'exercising' the dogs. One of his favourite games was The Hunt. It was easy to play, he'd been breeding rabbits in one of the outhouses especially for this diversion. He would take one or more of the rabbits and let the dogs have a sniff of them, then let them go a short way into the woods,

"Go get 'em me beauties!" The terrified creatures scampered off and often ran the bulky dogs ragged before escaping, but Kelvin always had another one to hand, one that he let go on the lawn for them to tear to pieces.

He stood legs apart with a shotgun under his arm, the dogs at his side whined and tugged at their chains eager to get on with the game,

"Easy boys, not long now, me beauties." He always

120

referred to the insane beasts as his beauties, except when in mid-hunt, then they became his Terminators.

Pretty soon the hunt was on, the dogs let loose they raced across the lawns towards the forest, snapping at each other in their eagerness to be first to the kill. Kelvin produced a torch from his waxed jacket pocket and ran quickly behind them. This time it was over in a few moments, in an attempt to avoid the leading dog the rabbit doubled back straight into the path of another. In a second, two of the dogs bit into it at the same time and neither of them would let go, Kelvin watched as they threw their heads from side to side in an effort to shake each other off, the rabbit was ripped to pieces and Kelvin had to step back quickly to avoid being sprayed with its blood.

He laughed, but was also disappointed that it was over so quickly.

*

Franco stood gazing out of the library window, Raven had just blown into the room like the beginning of the mad March winds,

"Those twins just make me die!" She said, taking up position next to him. He smiled gently,

"They are, erm, unique." He muttered as she left his side and breezed out of the room.

Franco was worried, lately he had begun to feel the heavy weight of old age, he had resisted it for so many years that when it finally came it came as a shock. He was worried that there would be no one to look after Raven when he was gone. He had always assumed that one day a younger man would come and take his position. There had been a couple of contenders but Franco had seen them off, now he began to feel that it was time to consider stepping down. He held up his hands in front of his face, he could picture the blood on them, but despite all he had done, he felt neither guilt nor shame. The world was a shitty place full of shitty people and they all got what they deserved. He smiled grimly to himself remembering when he had held Raven in his arms all those years ago, once he was a child to her, then her lover, now he felt more like a father to her. And of course above all else, he still loved her.

His gaze settled on a small group of crows waddling across the lawns, pecking and cawing, swaggering like black knights amongst peasants.

*

The twins finally left him alone and Richard breathed a huge sigh of relief, only to be startled seconds later as Cairo appeared from behind the wardrobe,

"I thought they'd never leave." She spoke quietly with a frown.

"How long have you been hiding there?!" Richard asked indignantly.

"Long enough, I guess they must like you very much. The way they kept touching you." Richard felt hot, embarrassed, it was clear to him that the twins wanted to start a physical relationship and he was trying to put them off without losing favour,

"You shouldn't spy on people." He still believed the twins were his best hope of escape. Cairo sat herself on the edge of his bed,

"I've never heard them talk so much." Richard nodded, a half smile,

"You know they're completely barking mad, don't

122

you?" Cairo giggled and nodded,

"Gosh yes…" She remembered something she'd overheard in the kitchen, "…Madder than a marshmallow, Fidelma says." Richard laughed, Cairo smiled. He felt the need to try to explain his behaviour,

"I only put up with them in the hope that they will help me to get out of here."

Cairo looked down, her face in shadow and hard to read,

"So you don't actually like them?"

"Like them? Ha! That's funny…" He rattled his chain, "…They've got me chained up like a pet dog in an attic somewhere, why the hell wouldn't I like them?"

Cairo raised her face, looked thoughtful before replying, the image of the dead bird in her mind,

"I have to go…" She turned and fled behind the wardrobe, "…But I'll be back soon."

Susan, Norfolk

After getting rid of the Vicar Susan pinned a large piece of paper to the front door,

'NO VISITORS'

She closed the door with a sigh of relief and the old cottage fell very quiet around her.

"First things first…" She told herself and shoved the cardboard box into the under stairs cupboard, "…Junk the junk-mail…" She fetched a plastic bin-liner and stuffed it full of the flyers, leaflets and local newspapers, "…That's better already." the hallway was empty.

She lumped her suitcase up the stairs and flopped it on her bed, then crossed the landing to her father's study which overlooked the back garden. She hoped to find information about Raven, and even possibly some clues to her whereabouts. At first sight it seemed an impossible task because most of his papers were in a terrible jumble. During the last few months of his life he had written a great deal, unfortunately most of it was written while he was roaring drunk and made little or no sense, and none of it was filed in any kind of logical order.

She sat herself down with a sigh, but once she'd got started she lost track of time, and so it was several hours later of sorting through the junk before she began to get things in order. Eventually she flicked on the light switch because she could no longer see properly and something at the back of her mind told her that it must be getting dark outside, she realised that she was dead tired and hungry.

With a yawn she wandered downstairs into the kitchen, with a thick pile of papers clutched in her left hand she pulled open the fridge door, it was completely empty. She had better luck in the food cupboard where she found a packet of chocolate digestive biscuits, only two months past their 'Best before' date, and some tins of soup. She settled for a mug of tomato soup which she sipped in front of the television.

After a few minutes she fell asleep.

She found herself climbing the stairs, a light was on in her parent's bedroom, the door was closed and the stairs unlit but enough light escaped from under the door for her to see by.

Hesitantly, she turned the handle and pushed open the door. The bedside lamps revealed the bodies of her parents laying next to each other in bed, a white sheet drawn up to their necks. Their eyes closed and their skin the colour of moonlight. Without warning they sat up straight, arms limp at their sides, the sheet falling to their waists. With a click their eyes snapped open and they glared accusingly at her. To Susan's mounting horror her father lifted a skeletal arm and pointed at her face, he shouted in a voice as cold and hard as death,

"You! Hide-away daughter! What do you want here? You're not welcome here! Get away from us! Stay away from us!" Then her mother raised her blotchy arms, covered her eyes with pallid fingers and began to scream, a long mournful wail that brought tears to Susan's eyes. Her father continued to rant,

"Get out of our house! And stay out! You're not wanted here. Get out get out get out!" The shouting and screaming continued as Susan backed trembling and sobbing out of the room, their clamouring din loud in her ears as she fled down the stairs.

She awoke with a wail, shaking, still in the armchair in front of the television. The dream had upset her and she dabbed at the tears blurring her vision, and at first she thought that it was all true, that the ghosts of her parents really did want her out of their house, and that they despised her. Then gradually as the power of the dream faded she began to reason, it was probably just her own guilt complex revealing itself in her dreams.

It takes a lot of courage to face one's nightmares; but Susan did it immediately, she rose and climbed the stairs, unable to stop the trembling in her fingers as she gripped the banister rail.

Pale light showed under her parents' bedroom door, her hand felt clammy on the handle. After a deep breath she pushed the door open. Her eyes darted immediately to

125

the bed, it was empty.

"Sheesh!" She hissed quietly in relief, glancing around the room. The curtains were open and the light that she'd seen had come from the brilliant moon outside. Everything appeared quite normal. She walked into the room, briefly glanced out of the window and closed the curtains, sitting on the bed she took stock of what she'd just achieved. She'd faced up to her ghosts, it was probably the most courageous thing she'd done in her entire life.

The house in the Countryside ~ 2000

At around the same time of night, but half the country away, Richard was awoken by Cairo lightly touching him on the cheek,

"I've come to help you escape!" She whispered loudly as she held up a small hacksaw in front of his face. He grinned and reached out to take it, noticing in the dim light that she was wearing lipstick and clumsily applied green eye-shadow.

"You little treasure." He murmured, but to his surprise she quickly pulled the hacksaw back from him and held it of his reach,

"Will you ever come back...?" She dropped her gaze and began to saw, "...To see me?" Richard only just caught her words,

"Yes. I'll be back. You can count on it!" But it was revenge on his mind, not a social call. The chain was cut and she stepped back as he rose and stretched, taking his hand she led him through the little door behind the wardrobe into her dark domain. It was hard to see, so she kept hold of his hand, it was too narrow for them to move two abreast in the tiny corridors and Richard had to stoop

126

many times to avoid bumping his head. After several short corridors she opened a door that turned out to be hidden behind a tapestry leading into a large bedroom vividly illuminated by the moon. The silver light cast deep shadows giving the room a black-and-white appearance. Without pausing, Cairo hopped over the window balcony,

"Don't worry, it's quite safe." She whispered. Richard peered dubiously over the parapet and gingerly lowered himself to the bough. At the heart of the tree, near to the trunk, Cairo had hollowed out a kind of den; she made Richard sit down on a bum-polished branch then sat facing him.

"We haven't much time." He reminded her.

"I know. I..." She wanted to say something, "...I'll probably never see you again." Richard suddenly felt desperately sorry for her, realising how bizarre and tragic her short life had been. He wanted to say something, but he didn't know what,

"You will see me again, I promise, I am coming back." He tried to reassure her but it was clear that she didn't believe him,

"I'm young and silly, but I'm not stupid." They were quiet for a few moments before Cairo spoke again,

"I'll be alone again. And it's going to feel different, isn't it?" Richard could not think of anything to say, and then in the gloom she leaned forward and took his hand again,

"It's time for you to go." She showed him the rest of the way down, near to the bottom Richard pulled her towards him and hugged her tightly,

"Thank you." He said and he dropped to the ground. A second later he was running for the trees. Cairo watched with sadness in her big eyes, *"Don't step on the shadows!"*

127

Across the lawn Kelvin Bright stood in his bedroom window, wearing only his camo boxers, he'd had a restless night and decided to smoke a cigarette before trying to get back to sleep, he hadn't bothered to switch on the light opting instead to pull back the curtains. He'd taken only one draw on his roll-up when he saw Richard drop out of the tree,

"Wha' tha fuck!" In the space of a heartbeat he whirled around and reached for his shotgun, as always it was loaded. With his cigarette held between his teeth he dashed out of his bedroom, out of the house to where the dogs were kept, they must have smelled him approach because they were awake and alert already, he fumbled with their chains setting three of them free,

"We got ourselves a prowler..." He hissed excitedly, "...See 'im off! go on, See 'im off me beauties!" The dogs enjoyed the game and jumped up and down in their excitement, they sensed blood and could smell the sweat from Kelvin, and as soon as the gate was open they leaped forward into the garden eager to bring down their prey.

Richard had wasted no time after dropping out of the tree, he ran straight in to the nearby woods intent on getting as far away as quickly as possible. He hadn't heard Cairo call out,

"I will miss you!" And neither did he see her drop to the ground a few moments later. She wandered sadly away from the tree, listlessly stepping over the shadows as Kelvin's dogs bore down on her.

Cairo was drawn from her melancholy reverie when she heard the dogs' snarling approach, her eyes widening in sudden fear as their black forms raced across the lawn towards her. She knew instantly that there was nowhere to run. In silent resignation, she put her hands in front of her face and braced herself to be torn to pieces.

From his hideaway in the hedgerows Mr Underhill had seen everything, and at the sight of the dogs he exploded from cover and raced to Cairo, arriving a second before the slavering beasts, pushing Cairo behind him.

He planted himself in front of her, legs apart, his head jutting forward and roaring at them, weaving his huge balled fists in front of himself. The animals were startled at his sudden appearance, but their confusion lasted only moments, they simply changed targets from Cairo to him, and as-one they leapt upon him.

Cairo gasped in surprise at the sound of Mr Underhill's roaring, she saw his back, broad and strong, buckle under the weight of the dogs' ferocious onslaught. His right fist slammed down on the head of the middle dog knocking it down to the ground, but the other two both penetrated his guard, biting him deeply in the thigh and shoulder, the middle hound quickly recovered and launched itself at Mr Underhill's throat. Cairo involuntarily clutched her own throat as she saw Mr Underhill catch the animal by the neck just inches from his face.

Kelvin was only a few seconds behind his beloved dogs with his shotgun at the ready, his heart nearly stopped when he saw Cairo about to be mauled, and he was equally astonished to see Mr Underhill appear out of nowhere to try to save her,

"Oh shit! Oh shit! Stop!…" He cried out desperately, "… Heel! Heel!" He was in a panic and could not get the dogs to stop their attack, they had the taste of blood on their

129

tongues and had been trained not to stop until they had killed. Mr Underhill had sunk to his knees under the attack but fought back by swinging the middle hound around in front of him like a giant living club. Wary of him now, the other two began to circle around him, snapping and snarling, looking for a weakness.

The noise and commotion had woken most of the household and it was Franco who was next on the scene, he strode quickly into the fray and without a seconds hesitation pulled out his small pistol and shot one of the dogs in the head. Kelvin was horrified,

"No! No! Don't kill 'em!" Kelvin stupidly rushed towards Franco with his shotgun still raised, he didn't have any intention to use it, he simply wasn't thinking clearly, Franco of course didn't know that and with blinding speed he pushed aside the barrel of the shotgun and smashed Kelvin in the face with the butt of his pistol knocking him out cold. The dogs, seeing their master in danger, turned their attack on to Franco. He shot twice in quick succession, both animals fell instantly. The attack was over.

Cairo immediately ran to Mr Underhill, feeling his pain like a sweet ache,

"Oh thank you..." She touched his shoulder gently, "... Oh but you're hurting so much." She saw the look of devotion in Mr Underhill's eyes but much more surprisingly to her, she felt it too. She closed her eyes and shuddered as the twin waves of his pain and his love washed through her mind.

Franco appeared at their side, he took Mr Underhill under the arm saying,

"Come, we must get you inside." He helped the limping man towards the kitchen, lights came on as they approached and Fidelma appeared in the doorway,

"And what in th' cursed seven bells of hell has gone on here!..." She crossed herself as she saw the awful bites, "...I knew it! Those devil-creatures should've been put-down years ago..." She took Mr Underhill's other arm and helped him towards a chair in the kitchen, "...Let me have a good look at those..." She cursed several more times, then, "...I hope your Tet'nus jabs are up to date my man..." He nodded, grimacing as she began to clean out his wounds, "...No doubt those beasts carried more than a deadly dose o' lockjaw!"

The twins arrived,

"We heard a commotion..." They announced as they entered the room, then gasped in tandem, "...We'll fetch our sewing kit..." They wheeled about, "...Back in a moment. Make the patient as comfortable as you can."

Raven eventually appeared while the twins were carefully sewing Mr Underhill back together, she joined Franco in the garden, where he held a blubbering Kelvin in an arm lock,

"I thought 'e was an intruder, ow!..." Kelvin whined, implying that none of it was his fault, "...How was I to know? A person shouldn't be hanging around the garden at night, ow...!" Franco gave him another little twist, "...Even if 'e is a bleedin' gardener! Ow!"

Cairo appeared at her mother's side, stating flatly,

"He set his dogs on me mother." Raven's eyes gave nothing away, Kelvin shrieked in terror,

"No! Never! No ma'am, not me, it was someone else!~" He was about to say that he'd seen a man drop out of the tree but Franco had heard enough from him, he punched him on the side of the head, and Kelvin was unconscious again. Raven's face was a mask, but her voice held deadly intent,

131

"Get him inside Franco, keep an eye on him..." She turned, took Cairo's arm, "...Don't let him leave the house alone..." She called over her shoulder, "... Make him take his dogs down to the pigs..." She led Cairo back towards the house. They were entering the kitchen before she appeared to notice Cairo's lipstick and eye shadow, she frowned,

"I'm not even going to ask."

Richard on the Run

Richard had continued running through the tangled forest all night, having heard the dogs barking and the gunshots in the distance he naturally assumed that they were after him, it never occurred to him that Cairo might have been in danger.

Just before dawn he crashed through some bushes and staggered into a road. There was no indication which way to go so he took pot-luck and turned left. A short while later he saw a small house at the end of a short shingle drive. His first instinct was to run up to it and bang on the front door, half way up the drive paused and took stock of his situation. Dawn was just breaking on a cold misty morning, the occupants of the house would almost certainly still be in bed. He looked down at himself, his shirt and jeans were torn and dirty from his flight through the woods, undoubtedly he was a mess. He reasoned that if he woke the people of the house they probably wouldn't let him, but instead would call the police. For some strange reason he did not want that to happen. He had been kidnapped and his wife probably murdered but he did not want to tell the police.

"So what the fuck am I going to do?" He whispered out loud to himself. He had no money and no transport.

Without realising it he had turned around and walked past the house. Then he continued walking. Gradually it became lighter, cars and lorries drove past him, and he passed more houses until he reached a town sign, 'Welcome to Shillingham'. Freezing cold and utterly exhausted he stumbled into the small town centre and slumped wearily in a shop doorway resting his head against the glass, within seconds he was asleep in a pale faint.

Walther, London

Walther allowed his head to drop back onto the hospital pillow and let out a discontented sigh. He had just been interviewed by the police for the third time in as many days, they wanted to know where Richard was and why Susan was now missing. It was obvious that they did not believe him when he said he had no idea of the whereabouts of either of them, even though he was telling the literal truth. At first he was relieved to find out that Susan had been discharged from hospital with only superficial face wounds (they hadn't told him the exact nature of the lacerations) but he became more worried when the police revealed that she was officially 'missing'. He became even more agitated when they informed him that Richard and Susan were both wanted 'in connection' with the death of someone named Smokey Dick, whose body was found to have traces of both Walther's and Susan's blood on it. It was obvious to the police that Smokey Dick was the one who had attacked Susan and Walther at her home, but what they could not work out was why he had done it and

"Why did he turn up dead so soon afterwards?"

After the third interview Walther discharged himself from the hospital, the doctor called him a fool but was unable to stop him leaving. With his head stitched and bandaged and every muscle in his body aching, he walked painfully to the nearest Underground Station. He sat on the train not noticing the curious glances of the other passengers, locked in a world of guilt for allowing Richard and Susan to become involved, *"I've been so stupid."* He berated himself while becoming more determined than ever to track down that angel of death called Raven.

He made his way across the city to Susan's house where he'd left his car, he was relieved that it hadn't been stolen or vandalised. He approached the front door to the house, the street was quiet and he could hear the phone ringing inside. It remained unanswered. He knocked on the door anyway, as he expected there was no answer so he quietly made his way around to the back of the house. He was astonished to find the back door unlocked. It had remained that way since Raven let herself out on the night of the attack. Cautiously Walther stepped inside, he walked slowly all over the house and could tell by the letters on the mat and the fine dust on places like the kettle and the toilet that no one had used the house for several days. He checked the wardrobes and noted that Susan's underwear and most of her make-up were gone, he came to the conclusion that Susan had probably left of her own free will,

"But where are you now?" He asked himself. He stood still and closed his eyes, trying to put himself in her position. He remembered something she had said back on his father's boat, *"I just locked the door and never went back. It still belongs to me, but I don't know what sort of*

134

state it's in. All their research is still there. But don't ask me to go and get it. I couldn't." He nodded in understanding,

"You've gone home, haven't you? After all this time you've decided to go back home to your parents house, to get help from mum and dad." Remembering the conversation they had back on his boat, he knew that it must be very difficult for her to go back, instinctively he also knew that she would want to be left alone. He left the house and drove home to his boat in two minds about whether to try to contact her or not.

"No, she's far better off out of this horrible business, at least she's safe now."

The house in the Countryside ~ 2000

The twins had discussed their failure to properly seduce Richard and agreed that wearing more make-up would probably do the trick. Painted like dolls they unlocked the door and marched proudly into Richard's cell carrying his breakfast,

"You'll never guess what happened last night." Their cheerful words ended abruptly, with twin gasps they stopped dead, side by side, gazing at his empty bed. One head turned to the left as the other turned to the right searching the corners of the room, then both heads turned to face each other with identical looks of horror and confusion.

"He's…" The one started to say,

"Disappeared!" The other finished. The tray clattered to the floor, forgotten in the awful realisation that Richard had left them, tears streamed down their identical cheeks as they hugged each other for comfort, still stood in the middle of the little room. Some time later they realised

135

that they should tell Raven that he'd gone,

"She'll kill us!" Pip protested.

"And put us in the Asylum!" Emm darkly reminded her. Then, together, without saying a word to each other, they crouched down and started to eat the mess of breakfast on the floor, each one taking it in turns to eat a piece of the cold food until it was all gone, then they drank the beer that they always brought for him, passing the bottle wordlessly between each other until it was empty. It was Emm who finally broke the silence,

"All gone! Richard seems to be getting quite an appetite these days!" She spoke to Pip as if Richard had eaten the breakfast, Pip replied,

"Yes, we shall have to speak to Cook about a larger portion for him!" The two mad girls collected up the things and left the room making sure that it was locked securely. They made every effort to avoid Raven over the next few days as they carried out their elaborate charade of pretending that Richard was still securely locked in his cell.

*

Cairo sat on the edge of the iron bed in Richard's attic room. The sawn-off handcuff was still attached. She slipped her hand inside, the metal felt cold and hard. She slipped out of it and rolled up her left sleeve. Then, from a pocket, she drew out the mother-of-pearl penknife she had stolen from the kitchen, opened out the blade, and drew it across her left forearm. The pain was exquisite. The blood beautiful. She held up her hand and watched it run down to her elbow and drip to the floor. And then she lay down and cried. Long silent sobs heard by nobody.

136

Richard, Shillingham

Richard woke with a start at the sound of a car horn, he shivered and blinked at the bright morning light noticing that there were pedestrians on the footpath and cars in the street. Shifting his cramped legs he knocked over a small pile of coins that were on the step beside him, he looked around in confusion until he heard a gentle tapping on the inside of the shop door behind him. He turned stiffly and saw an old lady peering at him through the glass, she pointed towards the coins and then made a 'shooing' gesture with her hands, Richard got the message and stood up. She had mistaken him for homeless and given him some money to go away, he picked up the coins and stumbled into the street.

After a few minutes walking Richard found what he was looking for; a public telephone. He dropped in some of the coins and dialled his home number, there was no answer. Next he dialled the office and was shocked to hear the 'disconnected' tone. In his mind he remembered Raven's parting words,

"Don't expect to see her pretty face again!" That was the moment when he realised that Susan really was gone, Raven had murdered her and boasted about it. A sudden rage overwhelmed him and he smashed the phone receiver against the wall, he kicked and punched the phone box tearing the skin off his knuckles until the frenzy was over. Staggering into the street he collided with another pedestrian, nearly knocking him over,

"Watch where you're fucking going!" He shouted, the other man walked away quickly, visibly nervous. Richard wanted to scream at everyone, to shout and punch

137

their smug, fatuous faces. He stood swaying on the footpath, glowering at the passers-by, wishing that someone would pick a fight with him. And then someone did. A large middle-aged uniformed policeman crossed the street and planted himself in front of Richard. His hand rested lightly on his truncheon.

"Fuck off!" Richard spat out the words and stared him right in the eyes. The policeman's eyes narrowed slightly but he didn't seem particularly annoyed, he spoke carefully and quietly with a hint of an Irish accent,

"You'd better be movin' on now, you 'travellers' are not welcome around here. This is a nice quiet respectable little town, and we don't want any scum like you making a mess of the place, so turn around and hoof-it right back where you came from!" He took out his truncheon and tapped it lightly in his palm, adding,

"Your grubby friends are camped in the lay-by about a mile down that road." He pointed with his truncheon to a road leading out of town. Richard realised that the policeman had mistaken him for a crusty 'new-age traveller', all of a sudden he had the urge to tell the policeman who he was and what had happened to him,

"Listen to me..." He took a step towards him, "...I've been kidnapped!..." He blurted out the words sounding almost hysterical, "...No listen, I was held a prisoner by two crazy women! They chained me to an iron bed!" Richard realised that he sounded crazy. The policeman smiled, a mirthless grin on his mouth and hatred and disgust in his eyes,

"Are you sure it wasn't 'the aliens' who abducted you then? Or was it 'the little people'?" He asked sarcastically before raising his voice menacingly and waving his truncheon in Richard's face,

138

"Now get your fucked-up, drugged-up filthy carcass out of my town, go on move it!" Richard turned away and headed down the road, his anger had dissipated when he realised how foolish he appeared, he trudged out of Shillingham without any idea of what he was going to do, the hopelessness of his situation becoming more apparent with every weary step.

Walking like an automaton he plodded without thought. Gradually the houses gave way to fields and trees, and he saw an old-fashioned single-decker bus parked in a lay-by. An old woman sat in its doorway with a steaming mug held in both hands, on the grass nearby sat an Asian man tending a camp fire, he remembered the words of the policeman, *"Your grubby friends are camped in the lay-by about a mile down that road."* Richard was hungry and desperately thirsty, he approached the woman,

"Can you spare some water, please?" He asked hoarsely.

"Piss off scrounger!" She glared at him and spat on the floor, Richard recoiled, shocked, then tried again,

"Please! I'm desperate, all I want is a-" The old woman stood up, turned around and went into the bus closing the door in his face. Richard stood there for a moment, stunned, until the sound of another voice made him turn,

"Hey! If you want something from us then you have to be prepared to trade, go and fetch some more wood for this fire, then we might be able to trade you some water."

Richard could hardly believe that he had to barter for a drink of water but it seemed like there was no alternative, he wandered off the road into the trees picking up twigs and fallen branches. A few minutes later he returned to the camp with a bundle of firewood, the Asian man eyed the twigs critically before handing over a mug half filled with water,

"Sip it. You're dehydrated." His English was very good but he retained a far-east accent. Richard wondered if he was Chinese and was surprised when he answered his unspoken question,

"I was born in Japan." He said it as if Richard had actually asked the question, then continued,

"Now sit down before you fall down." The Asian had a powerful grip as he took Richard's arm and eased him down beside the fire. The heat from the flames felt good and the water was cool and refreshing. Richard shuffled backwards getting more comfortable leaning against a bush, he felt that he ought to say something,

"Thank you..." It seemed appropriate, he continued, "...Can I rest here for a little while? Just until I get a little strength back? I'm very tired."
The Asian looked a little surprised, then replied,

"Strength, my friend, does not 'come back', it is not a thing which comes and goes like the moon or a migrant bird, it is always with you. It is born in you, A man only needs to know his strength and when and how to use it."

The statement was wasted on Richard, he'd only meant to say that he was tired and would like to rest for a while, the Asian man kept talking,

"I am known as Tsuba..." He held out his hand, Richard wearily took it and was surprised again, the hand felt as strong as iron, "...You are welcome to stay here for a while, but if you want to continue to use the fire then you will have to fetch some wood, and some more sturdy pieces! These few twigs will not burn long." Tsuba pointed to the pile that Richard had collected and then at some others that, presumably, he or the old woman had collected earlier, Richard nodded and promised to fetch some more later. The warmth from the fire and the weak sunshine helped Richard to relax and in only a few short minutes he had fallen asleep.

Raven, on the prowl ~ Birmingham

Raven sipped from a bottle of American lager, she was in Birmingham, in one of its more fashionable nightclubs, and she was bored. Usually such places were a hotbed of emotional and sexual tension, tonight things were a little quiet, it was midweek and the club was only half full, the clubbers that were there seemed only half interested as well. She was about to grab Franco and leave when she heard the immortal words,

"So what's a pretty girl like you doing all on her own?" She turned and saw a moderately attractive middle-aged man beaming his best 'I'm here on business and I've got an expense account' smile. She teased him with a suggestive lick around the rim of her bottle before replying,

"I'm not alone any more, am I?"

Walther, London

Back on his boat Walther emptied his jacket pockets and found the letter that he'd picked up when he was in the Hammersmith house with Susan, he read it. The contents were irrelevant but Sir Clive's name on the front told him who owned the house and gave him the idea that he might also own another house elsewhere, where Raven might now be hiding. It was a small lead but one well worth pursuing, he used his phone to make an appointment with a local private detective. He had also decided to find Susan and remembering her parent's names and that they lived in Norfolk meant that he should be able to trace her quite easily. He had become convinced that she would be hunting Raven for personal revenge and he wanted to offer his help, *"It is the least I can do..."* Walther was getting back in the hunt and determined that this time he would succeed, *"...But I would not blame her if she..."* He smiled sadly as he thought of the foul language Susan seemed prone to, *"...told me to fuck off."*

Susan, Norfolk

After that first terrifying night in the house, Susan's dreams had not been troubled by the spectres of her parents, instead she had vivid nightmares about Richard, somehow she could not accept that he was dead, he was missing and that was all, she would find him and bring him home. Home to Norfolk. Not their own house in Windsor, that had to be put into the past, she would build a safe haven for him in her parents' old cottage.

She had adopted a new sin to carry the guilt for, she blamed herself for Richard's disappearance. And that meant that she had to find him, or at the very worst what had become of him, she anchored her life, and sanity, in that tiny house next to the church.

In the days that followed her arrival she had spent a lot of time reading through her father's and mother's writings, hoping for information about the woman called Raven. But all she'd found were a few notes in a diary regarding a 'mysterious woman' they'd met in Africa, there was nothing concrete, nothing as straightforward as an address or full name.

She hadn't left the house since her arrival and had been surviving on the little food parcels left for her by the Vicar, there was a note pushed through the letterbox on her second day which read,

My Dear Susan,

I've taken the liberty of collecting a few things together for you (look on the doorstep!) Please call me if there is the slightest thing I can do to help,

Yours truly, and with the kindest regards,
Vicar.

She was angry at first but then admitted to herself that she was being irrational. She peeked from the curtains until she was sure the coast was clear then took in the parcel, grateful and surprised when she saw the bottle of sherry,

"Vicar's tipple!" She laughed out loud for the first time in ages.

Raven, driving back to Sir Clive's House

Raven sat in the passenger seat while Franco drove them back to the big house in the countryside near Shillingham, she'd noticed that he'd been quiet and a little pensive during recent days,

"Franco, tell me, what's wrong? You've hardly spoken a word for days. What are you brooding about?" He paused for a few seconds trying to frame a reply, then spoke quietly,

"I'm not sure, I've just got that feeling, you know the

one, the one that tells you things are not as they should be."
He shrugged. Raven knew him well enough to know that
his hunches were usually worth taking note of,

"In that case you had better talk to me about it..." She
said, "...when a wily old fox like you gets the heebies there
must be something up."

"Okay, I will try to explain, No, I'll ask you the same
questions that I've been asking myself, lets see if you come
up with the same answers:

One - Who was the man you and Dick saw with
Bryant's wife?

Two - Why did they kill Joan?

Three - Why didn't they go to the police after you
killed Leach? And again when Bryant went missing?
After all, any normal person would have gone to the police
straight away, wouldn't they?"

They were both silent for a few seconds before Raven
answered,

"It must be me they're after." Her voice was soft,
thoughtful, Franco nodded in agreement, adding,

"That was my guess also." Raven pursed her lips in
thought,

"Do you think they'll try again?" She asked.

"Yes I do, I feel certain of it, otherwise we would
have heard from the police by now."

There was another few seconds thought then Raven
asked,

"So who do you think the 'other man' is?"

"Von Vohberg. Who else could it be?"

"He's dead!"

"He had children, two sons I believe." Franco pointed
out with quiet intensity. Raven threw back her head and
laughed,

144

"Ha ha! Of course. Now I see it, Von Vohberg's idiot offspring set out to carry on his father's heroic crusade." Raven suddenly fell silent, vividly recalling Walther's father, and his stubborn fight against the Nazis.

Richard, at the roadside Camp

Richard woke up when Tsuba gently shook him at the shoulder, he was surprised to find a blanket across his chest up to his neck,

"Here my friend, have another drink…" Tsuba offered him a steaming mug, "…And sip it, it's hot." He pressed the steaming mug into Richard's hand. Richard obediently sipped, the contents were warm, herbal and refreshing. He finished it in a few moments and got to his feet, he felt stiff but generally much better. He saw that Tsuba was cooking something in a large metal pot over the open fire, there was no sign of the old woman,

"Francesca is on the bus…" Tsuba nodded his head in the direction of the bus as he again seemed to read Richard's mind, "…She's not so bad, she has had problems."

"I'd better go fetch some more firewood." Richard offered. Tsuba nodded without looking at Richard, he was sprinkling some chopped leaves into the cooking-pot.

This time Richard's foraging was much more successful and he'd gathered up a decent stack of stout lumber, as he returned to the camp he noticed that the sun had gone behind a large mass of dark cloud and that the late afternoon was quite cold,

"Looks like it might be a cold night." He ventured in conversation. Tsuba just nodded again, he seemed to be concentrating on his cooking. Richard hadn't eaten for two days and fervently hoped that dinner would consist of

145

something more substantial than a pot of simmered leaves.

Tsuba eventually looked up and nodded approvingly at the heavier timber,

"That's good! Now you've paid for the use of the fire and blanket, what will you trade for some food?"

"What!" Richard was furious and threw the wood down in temper. Tsuba laughed as he continued stirring the pot,

"You look very hungry!" He called out cheerfully enough, but Richard's fuse was so very short and he blew his top,

"You know I haven't got anything! What the hell do you want for fucksakes? blood!?..." Spittle flew as he screamed at Tsuba's impassive face, "...Well you can keep your bloody food! Shove it where the fucking sun rises! I can live quite easily without a bowl of boiled hedgerow cuttings anyway!" He started to stamp away from the camp, and then he saw the bread. Tsuba had been baking unleavened bread on a flat rock at the side of the fire, it looked hot and delicious. Across the fire Tsuba again caught his eye, speaking as gently as ever,

"There is **something** you have for which we would be pleased to trade for a hot meal and a dry bed." Richard stopped, took a deep breath and asked,

"Like what?" Tsuba took no notice of Richard's harsh tones and replied almost jovially,

"Your story of course! I can see that you have been through quite an ordeal. We all have a story to tell, tell us yours. I have a hunch that it will be worth more than just one meal and a place to sleep." Tsuba grinned and beckoned Richard back towards the fire,

"You have a quick temper." He noted. Then they both heard the door to the bus open and saw the old lady

146

emerge with a large colourful shawl around her shoulders, she glowered at Richard and moaned,

"Why's 'e still 'ere?..." She asked of Tsuba as she pointed to Richard with her thumb, "...Can't yer get rid of 'im?" She sat herself down grumpily by the fire, warming her hands in front of its cheerful flames.

The house in the Countryside ~ 2000

Cairo sat at a small square wooden table in Mr Underhill's shack. He was making tea in his own large quiet manner, moving even more carefully to avoid aggravating his bite wounds. The shack consisted of a downstairs living room with a kitchen area at one end and a narrow wooden staircase that led up to the single bedroom, she wondered how he managed to get up such a tiny space. Almost every available shelf had a plant or flower on it as well as most of the floor space. The wooden walls of the shack blended in with all the foliage like flat tree trunks creating the atmosphere of a forest clearing on a still summer afternoon.

Sunlight peeked through the flowers of a pretty square window and Cairo watched leafy shadows dance on the rough-grained table top.

"Milk and sugar?" His voice was deep and sweet, like music from the bottom of a deep, wide wishing well.

"Yes please." Her own voice sounded small and soft in her ears. Since Richard had gone she had spent more time out of the house than in it, many of her usual haunts having been abandoned, she had even taken to sleeping in her bed instead of under it, mainly because she didn't want to talk to Button. She knew that she had changed inside but didn't know how much, the feelings that she had been

147

receiving from people had scared her at first and so she spent most of her time alone in the garden or with Mr Underhill. They hardly spoke but they felt quietly comfortable together.

He placed a china cup and saucer in front of her almost filled to the top with pale sweet tea, then, in the centre of the table, he placed a small terracotta pot in which a tiny white flower had just bloomed.

"I hope you like it. It's a species that I've crossed myself, I've named it Pure Cairo." She looked deeply into his eyes feeling his emotions without embarrassment, she felt an intense, warm passion radiating from him, a passion way beyond anger, fear or hate, she felt the passion of his love.

*

Raven stared at Richard's empty bed, it was obvious that it had not been slept in, the question was why? And for how long? She had no doubt in her mind that he had escaped and that the twins must know that he had gone. Had they helped him? She felt betrayed, and then angry. A white rage overwhelmed her, she flailed out of the little room in a whirlwind of bad temper, sploshed herself down the stairs like the boiling spew from a volcano.

Franco saw her as she steamed past the library heading for the kitchen, he could tell that something was going to happen and followed discreetly,

Raven boiled into the kitchen grabbing the little Irish cook by the shoulders,

"Where are they?!..." She was rolling out dough and dropped the rolling pin, "...Where are the stupid little bitches hiding?!" The little cook, although frightened,

148

could be quite feisty when angered, she shook herself free and shouted back at Raven,

"Well how th' divil should I know?..." She glared up at her, "...When all I do all day, to no t'anks from anyone, is slave is this blasted old kitchen! They could be half way up the road to Killarney for all I know! Or care!"

Raven picked up the rolling pin and contemplated bludgeoning her with it, she resisted the temptation, slammed it down, and marched out of the kitchen calling their names,

"Margaret! Philippa! Show yourselves!" She found them in the great entrance hall, they stood side by side in front of the door, they had their coats on and each held a large suitcase, their cheeks were tear-stained and they were clearly terrified. Emm spoke up first,

"We're ready to go~"

"~To the asylum." Pip finished in a thin wail, they moved slightly closer together and held hands. Without breaking stride Raven marched up to them and placed a hand on each of their heads then knocked them together, hard. The girls squealed and both fell to the floor clutching at their heads.

"How long has he been gone?" Raven demanded. The girls tried to reach for each other, too afraid to reply,

"Answer me, damn you!" They were sobbing and clutching each other, Raven pulled back her foot and kicked Emm hard in the face, knocking her backwards, her face quickly awash with blood.

The emotion emanating from the two girls was sending Raven into a frenzy, she was finding it almost impossible to hold herself back,

"You're not going to the asylum! That place is too good for you! I'm sending for Sir Clive..." She kicked Pip in

149

the ribs, "... You can join him in the cellar! Help him with his experiments..." She stamped hard on Emm's head, "...And then we can feed what's left of you to the pigs!"

The girls were howling with terror, the entire household lived in fear of Sir Clive, fear of what he did to those young women he took down to the cellar. Raven had Emm's arm twisted behind her back almost to the point of dislocation, she had succumbed to the frenzy. Franco's powerful voice broke through,

"Mistress!" He was probably the only living person who could bring Raven back, she let go of Emm's arm stood up and glared at him,

"They have betrayed us! And they will suffer for it!" She yanked Emm's bloody face up by her hair and pressed a finger into her eye, Franco interrupted her again,

"What have they done?" His voice was mellow as he tried to calm her.

"They've let him go!" Emm screamed and thrashed about.

"We didn't! We didn't! He just vanished!" Pip wailed as she tried to pull Raven's hand from Emm's face.

Franco thought quickly, he was pretty sure it would be a bad idea to kill the twins,

"Perhaps we should question them first?" He gently placed his hand on Raven's shoulder making her turn to face him. She paused for breath, seeing the sense in what Franco had said,

"Very well, bring them to the library!" He had bought them some time, some time for Raven to come to her senses he hoped. She marched ahead, catching a glimpse of a sheepish Kelvin Bright before he ducked back out of sight,

"I'll be seeing to you one day soon as well! *Cocky*

little shit..." She said to herself, promising something uniquely painful for his ultimate demise, "*...Where did I leave those thumbscrews?*"

Chapter 5
"And for all I've done..."

Richard, a lay-by near Shillingham

"I said, can't you get rid of 'im?" The old hag repeated petulantly, still wagging her grubby thumb towards Richard.

"Bad enough 'avin' you to look after! Can't afford a free ride for every sponging no-good what walks into me camp! Ain't you got that food ready yet?" Richard watched the grumpy old bag as she pulled out a small glass bottle from somewhere beneath her layers of soiled clothing, he guessed that it contained Gin or something similar. She took a quick swig and coughed wheezily before continuing her rant,

"An' 'e ain't 'avin' none o' my 'winter warmer' neither! I needs it for me chest!" She took another short swig from the bottle of 'winter warmer' and fell into a fit of wheezing and coughing, obnoxiously blind drunk.

Tsuba watched her sympathetically then glanced at Richard, shaking his head gently he spooned out a portion of broth into a bowl that had been warming by the fire, he passed it over to her. Richard noticed a very strong herbal aroma as the bowl passed by and guessed correctly that Tsuba deliberately added them to the broth to ease the old lady's chest complaint. She held the bowl under her nose for a few moments before eating to allow the vapours to circulate, her wheezing eased a little. Richard found himself wondering how the odd couple had come together, perhaps they had a story to tell even more bizarre than his own.

153

Richard was next to receive a bowl of the steaming aromatic broth together with two pieces of the flat bread,

"Thanks." He said. Tsuba smiled showing a white set of teeth.

"After eating you must entertain us with your story, and please, do not try to shorten any of it, start at the very beginning and leave nothing out!" Tsuba loaded up the fire after they'd eaten and then sat down to listen to Richard's story.

"I really don't know where to start." Richard shook his head, just a little embarrassed.

"Begin with your name, or what you would like us to call you, then tell us what you were doing just before the misfortune fell upon you, the one that has left you so alone in this world that you have to wander the streets begging for food and shelter."

Falteringly at first, and with many backtracks, Richard told his tale. He told them how happy and simple his life was with Susan and how quickly it all changed after Raven had walked into his print shop. Tsuba was greatly interested in her and asked many questions, often making Richard go back to explain something in more detail. Towards the end of his narrative Richard noticed that darkness had fallen, the old hag appeared to be asleep and a cold drizzle had started, making the parts of his clothes that were not facing the fire quite wet. Tsuba carefully placed more wood on the fire saying,

"A truly marvelous tale..." He said, "...And one that a great many people would find impossible to believe." Richard shrugged as if he didn't care whether Tsuba believed him or not,

"I'm still hungry..." He said, adding sarcastically, "...Have I earned enough entertainment points for some

154

more of that soup?"

"Yes indeed, a fine story like yours is worth a dry bed for the night, and some breakfast at least!" Tsuba handed over another bowlful before adding more seriously,

"You have given me much to think about. Many years ago, when I was in Cambodia..." He frowned at the memory, "...I met a woman such as you describe, the one that goes by the name Raven she came on a wave of great evil in that country. She herself..." His voice trailed off, remembering much more than he wanted to tell, "...Was not evil, somehow she brought out the latent evil in others, there were many deaths, many atrocities. We, I, er-" Tsuba trailed off lost in thought while Richard ate his soup. It was a few minutes later that Richard noticed that the fire was almost out, he hastily bundled on the last of the collected wood.

"I suppose I should fetch some more wood if we're to keep this fire going." He didn't receive an answer, The old woman still appeared to be asleep and Tsuba was gazing, trance-like, into the darkness,

"I didn't realise my story was that exciting. Sent him into a coma." Richard muttered to himself as he again trudged back into the woods, it took a little while for his eyes to adjust to the darkness and he had to go further to find suitable pieces of timber. The drizzle was persistent and cold, he was shivering by the time he got back to the camp and was relieved to see that the fire had not quite gone out, he dropped his load and knelt in front of the tiny fire to gain some of its warmth. Tsuba had awoken from his trance and was busy setting up some kind of screen around the fire. It was a kind of open-ended tent woven out of slender branches that when positioned around the fire would protect it from the rain and excessive winds but

155

would also allow it enough air for it to burn properly. Richard was quietly impressed. When the 'tent' was in position Tsuba quickly started sorting through the timber that Richard had fetched, some of it he placed immediately onto the fire, the rest was stacked neatly inside the 'tent' to dry out,

"We have to keep the wood as dry as possible." He muttered by way of explanation. Richard turned at the voice of the old hag,

"'ere, 'ave this!..." She threw a dark pile to the ground. "...Though you don't deserve it, scrounger!" Without further comment she spat on the ground and returned to the sanctuary of the bus. Richard ignored her and whatever it was that she'd thrown down. Tsuba spoke next, he sounded slightly embarrassed.

"We've got this sleeping tent you can use... It should keep you dry..." He moved to the dark pile and started undoing straps before adding, "...If you can keep the fire going through the night we can all have a hot breakfast, with this rain I doubt if I could get a fire started before we set off tomorrow."

"Okay, thanks." Tsuba smiled and busied himself erecting the tiny sleeping tent. Richard was tired and grateful for the things that he had got, a fairly dry place to sleep, a fire and some food in his belly, *"It Could be a lot worse..."* He told himself, *"...Tomorrow I'll move on."* And although he still had only the slightest idea of where he was or what tomorrow might bring he fell asleep almost instantly.

The house in the Countryside ~ 2000

In the great kitchen of the old house Anjelica and

156

Fidelma sat at a bare wooden table playing cards, as they often did when it was late and the house was quiet. Anjelica, popularly nicknamed Jelly, laid down her cards, almost knocking over her tall glass of sherry,

"There's evil in this house." She slurred.

"To be sure..." Fidelma agreed in her rich Irish Brogue, "...But tis nothin' to do with us, we're just the 'help' around the place." Jelly took a large swig of sherry and, still clutching the glass and swaying slightly from side to side, made the assertion,

"Yes, and that's as maybe, but we're also the one's who're going to need some 'help' sooner or later! Mark my words! That bitch is crazy!" She tapped the side of her head for emphasis. Fidelma understood that she was referring to Raven,

"To be sure, I don't disagree wid you, she's as mad as a brush. But she's not the one we have to guard ourselves against, the real evil goes on down there!..." She pointed to the floor, "...Down in that mad hell-hole of a cellar, in that so-called laboratory!..." She dealt new cards before continuing, "...tis that poor little Cairo I feel sorry for, what kind of a life is she going to have? Living in this house full of nutcases, neglected like a poor little orphan-child."

At that moment the bruised and sorrowful twins filed into the room wearing their nightdresses,

"We're..."

"Hungry." They said. Fidelma and Jelly exchanged knowing glances and a shake of the head before Fidelma replied,

"Well, you're not helpless are yer? Your arms'r not broken are they? You know where everything is. Help yourselves, just don't be leaving a mess behind you!"

They continued to play cards in silence while the

157

twins raided the larder,

"I want cake."

"And cheese."

"And crisps!"

Fidelma rolled her eyes at Anjelica, she smiled and tapped her forehead whispering,

"They're harmless really."

Susan, Norfolk

Churchyard trees dripping with pink blossom overhung the garden wall at the back of the little Norfolk cottage, a gusty spring wind brought down cascades like confetti turning the newly mown lawn pink.

Susan, out of breath, put down her skipping rope for a few minutes to enjoy the beautiful sunny morning. Tommy Paston had been in the garden the day before, mowing the lawns and tidying up the windblown debris. Susan remained inside, occasionally peeking through her bedroom curtains. He looked pretty much the same as she remembered, except, of course, a few years older. He had glanced up at the house from time to time but made no effort at contact.

Susan was grateful for that. She had found the skipping rope and her old exercise bike amongst the things still stored in her former bedroom, she remembered when, as a teenager, she had been a bit of a keep-fit fanatic. Looking at her body, instead of her face for a change, she realised that she had let it go a little and decided to work-out again. Setting herself a routine that included skipping, cycling, sit-ups and press-ups she found that the physical exertion worked wonders for her moods, she felt less angry after a good work-out and more able to cope with her depression. As the lonely days passed she regained her former athletic figure and laughed one morning when her, once tight fitting, jeans slipped down off her hips, she had to find a belt to hold them up. She'd also stopped looking at her face in the mirror all the time, the exercising had been good therapy for her.

And so it came as something of a shock to her when a few days later she looked into the bathroom mirror to see that the scabs had fallen from her face leaving only faint pink lines. By looking closely she could still read the carefully cut letters SLUT but she knew, knew deep inside with intense relief, that they would fade further and might be completely hidden by a little make-up. She saw her eyes grow sparkly before her sight was blurred by a flood of warm wet tears, tears of gratitude that the ugly word had gone. Soon, she knew, that she would be able to go out into the world again.

Later that day, after her workout, while she was poring over yet more of her mother's writings, she came across a name and an address, the name was Sir Clive and the address was the same as the house she and Walther had raided in Hammersmith, her excitement grew further when she saw that there was another address for Sir Clive, apparently he had a house in the country near a town called Shillingham. Her mother described Sir Clive as:

"A charming and vigorous man on the outside, but beneath his facade he was one of the most insanely evil men I have ever known." Susan read a little further, then without consciously thinking about it, she went to the phone and dialed a number, it was answered quite quickly,

"Good afternoon, how may I help you?"

"Walther! Is that you?"

"Yes, who-"

159

"It's Susan! Listen, I've got an address!" She quickly checked her watch before continuing, it was almost half past two,

"I'll be at the boat by seven! Put the coffee on!" She slammed down the phone as a triumphant and determined grin forced itself across her face,

"Now for some payback time!" She shouted out loud as she started to gather some things together. Only a few minutes later she was running out of the house to her car.

The house in the Countryside - 2000

Raven had only arrived back in England a few weeks earlier. She had been in and around Congo and Rwamda for the previous five years, feeding on the miseries of the terrible bloody war. She was finding it difficult to adjust to life in England.

She switched off the television with a snarl as the closing music to Eastenders began,

"I hate the way they glorify such depressing ugliness..." She threw the remote control onto a side table, "...Millions of people, and not just the fat slovenly plebs, watch that dross every day, glued to it, convinced that it's good to be that stupid, that..." She struggled to find the words, "...That, common!..." She rose and glowered at the now blank screen, "...Those people, those caricatures of the ugly and selfish side of humanity..." She waved a dismissive hand towards the set, "...Are their role-models!..." She shook her head in disbelief, sighing, "...For the sake of the Walking Woman! They actually want to **be like them**..." She fought against the urge to wrestle the TV set to the ground and forced herself to calm down, "...Still, I suppose peasants will always be peasants, whatever century they're

160

in."

Franco was busy taking a lot of no notice of her. He was used to reactional ranting, every time she switched on the television she ended up losing her temper with either the presenters or the presented, she despised the mundane. He understood why. She had no time for passive entertainment, she'd never been able to just sit still and enjoy, even his beloved Barbieri failed to keep her attention, she needed to be a part of a live situation, clapping, cheering, dancing. Fighting. He recalled the look on her face at the Pamplona Bull run. So happy and full of vigour. He sighed as she continued her pointless rant,

"I am so sick of this petty, narrow~minded hypocritical little country! I need some fresh air, from a free country, a country without ID. cards, without video cameras in the high streets and without your life history stored away on a stupid computer!" Franco shook his head gently and smiled, softly interrupting her he said,

"Why don't you take out one of the horses? The ride might make you feel better."

She turned on him quickly and for a split second he wondered what she might do, then she favoured him with her best *"I've been ranting again haven't I?"* smiles and skipped towards the door,

"I think I will!..." She said, adding as she glided out of the room, "...And I might trample down a few gurning peasants while I'm at it!"

Franco waited until she was out of earshot,

"I doubt you'll find many people outside, mistress, peasants or otherwise, they will all be indoors, glued to their TV sets, paralyzed by the soaps." With a wry smile he returned to his game of chess.

Raven, galloping amidst the blossom trees

She rode hard. The horse was panting when she pulled up beneath a canopy of white blossom. Petals fell around her like snow, triggering a long-forgotten memory:-

Christmas in Victorian London.
Late at night, Raven gazed through the drawing-room window at a gas-lit cobbled street below, snow fell thick and soft,
"It's settling." Her voice a solemn whisper. The house was quiet but for the occasional crackle of the log fire, she was in a polite area of old London town, far away from the urchins and the scurrying rats. But she was alone. The master of the house, her current benefactor, and a doctor of some conscience, had been called away to tend to the ailing children of a wealthy wool merchant. The servants had retired for the night, it was all too quiet. She turned from the window, her gaze falling to the musical box, she sat, pulled it onto her lap and turned the little clockwork handle. She closed her eyes as it began to play.
When the music stopped she opened her eyes, and blinked in disbelief. The room had changed, the luxury curtains and furnishings had gone, the fireplace was empty, and a chill wind blew snow through a broken window pane. She rose in haste, sending the musical box clattering to the floor. Taking the candle holder she stepped from the room, her shoes echoing on bare floorboards. She scurried down the stone steps to the kitchen, empty, the hearth barren and cold. Footsteps from above made her turn, "There's someone in the hallway." She arrived in time to see a small shadowy figure climbing

162

the stairs to the first floor. She tried to speak, but words failed her as the entity stopped and turned, a young girl, her face a ghastly white, her eyes black sockets. She seemed to nod, then turned and resumed climbing the stairs, pale skeletal legs and rough boots knocking and scraping the bare wooden steps. Up ahead, from somewhere in the higher levels of the house, Raven could hear voices, a babble, a childish cacophony.

The skeletal girl had reached the landing and gone out of sight. Raven followed, cautious and curious, step by step in the candlelight to the top, where her foot brushed against something soft. Trembling, she peered down, "Just a teddy bear." Without thought she picked it up and took the next flight of stairs.

At the top she reached an open door, the childish babble loud inside. Children scampered around, some were broken, all were damaged in various ways. They milled around, a semblance of playing, one had no legs and sat with a paper doll. Another showed the pock-marks of disease, another burns. The blind skeletal girl circled and reached out but never found. A feral boy huddled in a dark corner, a baby lay dead beside him.

On some hidden cue they ceased their macabre parody of play to stand still, then turned to stare at Raven, their glares pathetic, heartbreaking.

"It can't be-" Suddenly knowing who they were, Raven dropped the teddy bear, gasping in grief and pain, her voice a hollow misery,

"The ghosts of all my children."

She woke as the mantelpiece clock chimed midnight, the musical box was still on her lap, the fire burned low, the snow continued to fall. On Christmas day.

Richard, the roadside Campsite

Richard had toyed with the idea of letting the fire go out and leaving the camp just before the others got up, a kind of petty revenge for their indifferent attitude towards him, fortunately good sense prevailed, it had been a cold wet night and he could do with a hot breakfast.

The morning was brighter than he had expected, the rain having blown away by dawn, he was astonished at how beautiful the forest looked in the early morning sunlight, and golden shafts penetrated the gloom as he tramped through the trees looking for more firewood. By the time he returned to the camp, Tsuba was up and busy at the fire,

"I was afraid you might have gone." Tsuba said in his phlegmatic eastern manner.

"Nearly did, thought I'd have breakfast first." Richard replied dropping his lumber.

"I'm glad you stayed." Tsuba said in a way that implied he wanted to say more.

"How come? Getting fed up with the old cow?" It was Richard's turn to wag his thumb. Tsuba smiled at Richard's jibe and replied,

"I want to help you." He had the fire going well again.

"Help me to do what exactly?"

"To find your enemy, the woman called Raven."

"And what makes you think I want your help?" Richard handed him some more wood for the fire.

"Ah. You see, my religion does not recognise the event you would call coincidence. It is my belief that we were meant to meet here. I was sent here to help you."

165

"Bollocks." Richard's reply was blunt. Tsuba was unmoved and continued unabashed,

"Listen, my brusque friend, hear me out. I have been travelling for many years, all around the world. And in all that time I wasn't just wandering, I was searching. I have taken many wrong turns, and it appears that luck has finally intervened." Richard's normally ferocious scepticism of all things mumbo-jumbo had taken a serious denting in recent days so he bit his tongue and let Tsuba continue.

"This place..." He waved his hand encompassing the scruffy lay-by, "...Is the appointed place where I was meant to join with you..." He reached into his jacket, "...Look at this." Tsuba took a slip of crumpled paper from an inside pocket, he unfolded it carefully and handed it to Richard, it was a photo.

"Taken in Cambodia many years ago, that is me third from the right." Richard looked closely at the crumpled black-and-white photo. He saw a group of soldiers cheering and waving their rifles in the air, a young man who looked like Tsuba among them. Behind and above the group was a Russian tank, stood up by the turret was an officer and to Richard's amazement, next to him, dressed in military combat gear and holding a pistol high above her head was Raven, unmistakably. Richard handed back the photo,

"It's her." He mumbled, amazed. Tsuba nodded,

"I hardly dared to believe, listening to your story, I thought *"It can't be her"* but during the night I remembered there are no coincidences, it **had to be her**."

"And how long have you been looking for her?"

"Sixteen, no seventeen years."

"Wow! It looks like you were fighting on the same

166

side, is that how you met?"

"No. Not at first. We er, met, in a village, I fought with the Khmer Republic, she was, er, more of a free-agent." Tsuba shook his head in a rueful smile,

"I was an idealistic boy. I knew no better. I grew up in Japan, naïve in a well-off family. Ran away to fight in a war in another country. Fighting. Until-" Tsuba ran out of words. Richard sensed there was something between him and Raven, and blurted out,

"So you and her, got it on together?" Tsuba ignored the question,

"Please believe me, Richard, there really are no such things as coincidences. And I am going to help you find her."

The house in the Countryside - 2000

The twins sat in their pink chintz bedroom clutching their dolls and staring at the wall. They had been let off. Raven had finally and begrudgingly accepted that it was not their fault that Richard escaped. But inside their mad heads something had been changed, an entirely new set of thoughts troubled their already overcomplicated minds. They felt a sense of loss at Richard's escape but they knew without thinking that they could cope with that, life moved on. It was the growing feeling of discontent with their lot that was upsetting them. All of a sudden they had lost their trust and dependence on Raven.

"She shouldn't have hurt you like that." Pip said gravely. She had always been the meeker of the two, but meekness does not necessarily mean weakness.

"I'll be all right." Emm replied as cheerfully as she could manage, hugging her sister with one arm. The other one was strapped to her chest and she had a bandage on her nose, the bags under her eyes were blue/black.

"She shouldn't've done it." Pip muttered again and continued to frown at the wall.

Walther's boat, London

Susan drove alongside the Thames towards Walther's boat, she was mildly surprised to see his garage empty with its doors open wide, his car was parked parallel to the boat on the riverside road, evidently he had been waiting for her and as she approached he waved her straight on into the garage.

"The police are looking for you!..." He explained while he quickly closed the doors to conceal her car, "...They want to talk to you about a murder."

"Who's been murdered?" Susan demanded, jumping to the wrong conclusion that it might have been Richard.

"Well, evidently, the man who attacked us at your home was killed later that very same evening. Obviously they know that it wasn't us that did it because we were both in hospital but, they still want to interview you about it and about Richard's disappearance. I think he might be their strongest suspect." While Walther was talking he led Susan onto the boat, all the while looking around to see if anyone was watching.

"Aren't you being just a little bit too melodramatic? And what's wrong with saying Hello?" Susan was amused at his over protective attitude. She stood in the centre of the cabin with her hands on her hips. Walther had been peering out of the window at the empty road outside. He turned to her with a small laugh at himself before replying,

"Yes I suppose I am being a little foolish. I'm sorry, It

168

is very good to see you. How are you? You're looking very, er, thin!" He had looked at her properly for the first time since she'd arrived and was shocked at how slim she had become.

"Thank you. I think..." Was her deadpan reply, "... you're looking pretty wasted yourself. Your face is still swollen."

There was an awkward silence which Walther suffered in embarrassment, Susan let him suffer even though she had not really felt offended. Finally she allowed him off the hook,

"Speaking of murder, I could kill for one of your coffees." She smiled, Walther smiled,

"Of course, how very remiss of me." and fled quickly to the galley. Susan was amazed at how in control she felt.

A little while later the atmosphere had relaxed, Susan had told him of her ordeal at the cottage, her scars and her fear. He had shown a great deal of concern about her face, even blaming himself for not protecting her well enough against Smokey Dick. He looked carefully at the thin scars and pronounced confidently that they would become more and more faint as time went by, eventually her story was told.

"And so what have **you** been doing?" She asked him over a second cup of coffee.

"Well my dear, I've certainly not been idle. I engaged the services of a private investigator and like you, I've also come up with an address!" He bubbled with enthusiasm as he related his plan,

"I had initially planned to drive up there and just have a snoop around. But then I had second thoughts, it might look too obvious, I might be seen. So I came up with the idea of approaching the house on the blind side! Let me

169

show you what I mean." He stood up, his head touching the ceiling, pulled open one of the polished wooden drawers and retrieved a map. Moving the cups to one side he spread the map over the table in front of them,

"See here, this is the town of Shillingham..." He pointed with the end of a gold pen, "...And here is the house..." Susan nodded waiting for him to get to the point, "...And this blue line..." He traced along it with the pen, "... Runs passed the house, I estimate no more than three hundred yards away, and all the way to here!" He lifted the pen from the map and pointed it theatrically at the floor of the boat. Susan's brow furrowed, not sure what he was alluding to. He quickly made his point,

"That thin blue line is the river Thames! We can sneak up on them by boat." He seemed very pleased with the idea, Susan smiled and thought about it.

"Yes..." She said finally. "...It is a good idea. In fact it's fucking brilliant, let's do it. We can leave tomorrow."

Richard, a roadside camp near Shillingham

Richard was not at all convinced by Tsuba's coincidence theory but he had to admit to himself that he could use some help, at least for the time being. And he'd seen so much crazy shit just lately he couldn't rule out anything. And so, slightly reluctantly, he stayed with Tsuba and the old woman. Tsuba immediately appointed himself as mentor to Richard and instigated a training routine to increase his fitness and mental awareness. Richard had not enjoyed being told that he was flabby and slack-minded but went along with the exercises as much to pass the time as for any other reason. And after the first few gruelling days while his muscles adjusted he found himself

170

enjoying the routines, even the ones that he had initially thought daft. And then one morning he realised that he actually did feel fitter, more flexible and more alert than he had ever felt before. Tsuba was pleased, Richard had responded well to the training.

They moved camp usually every one or two days, to avoid trouble with the locals or the police, but they stayed in the general area of Shillingham where Richard had walked out of the forest. They had pin-pointed the probable location of the house on one of Tsuba's maps and Richard was becoming impatient,

"For all we know she could be long gone, she could be in Australia by now for all we know!" Richard said testily over an evening meal. As was his way, Tsuba thought for a second before replying,

"Yes, she may have moved on. But we know where the trail starts, it starts at the house, we can always pick it up from there."

"No! Yes, I agree, but we've already wasted too much time already, we should strike now! I say we go tomorrow." Richard spoke forcefully, impatient as ever. And he was surprised at the reply he got from the mild mannered Asian,

"Okay. As you wish. You and I will approach the house tomorrow, undercover. We will make camp nearby and observe, only observe!..." He stressed the point before he continued, "...I have good binoculars. Then we will return here to make attack plan. Agreed?"

"Er, yes, great." Richard's mind went into a whirl, *"At last!"* he thought to himself. They retired early that night with the intention of making an early start in the morning. Richard's sleep had been relatively peaceful since he'd joined with Tsuba, the series of nightmares he'd been

171

suffering were largely forgotten, which left him totally unprepared, as everyone is, for the next one:

"Is the blindfold secure?"

"Yes." It was pitch-black, he couldn't see a thing, there were girls voices, they sounded familiar but he couldn't quite place them. He tried to move but couldn't, his arms and legs were held outstretched by cold metal clamps around his wrists and ankles. He was on his back.

"He's moving! Are the shackles on tight?"

"Yes."

Richard felt sticky tape pressed over his mouth, now he couldn't speak. Or scream. He was afraid, very afraid. In the blackness he felt a warmness close to his face, it got hotter. Instinctively his body tensed like a bowstring and he cringed away from the hot something. Then he felt a gentle pressure against his cheek and a soft gush of warm air. He'd been kissed.

"Goodbye my love." Said the first feminine voice.

"Goodbye." Gently echoed the other.

He felt himself being carried away as if he was on a plank or board. Then he heard the rolling of waves as if he was on a beach followed by the sound of splashing feet, he guessed that he was being led into the ocean.

"Farewell my love."

"Farewell."

Then he was floating on the sea, adrift. The voices had gone to be replaced by the sounds of the open sea, coarse winds and breaking waves. After a time he began to hear other sounds, less wholesome, hisses and gloops surrounded him, he pictured in his mind an army of hungry sea-beasts eager to take a bite out of his warm body. Then he felt cold, with mounting terror he realised that he was

172

naked. Suddenly he was startled as something landed on his chest, it had claws and it pecked him. Soon more creatures arrived to feast on him, he could feel their slimy bodies as they crawled out of the sea and onto his chest. He felt them nipping at him, all over his legs arms and chest. The creature with the claws had moved up to his face and began pecking at his cheek, Richard thrashed about as much as he could to try to dislodge the vile parasite but to no avail, more and then more of them clambered up out of the sea onto his raft covering him, and then more of them piling on top of each other in their desire to get to his flesh. Then he felt cold sea-water flood across the raft, the creatures were sinking it! They were taking him under the sea to feed on him!

Richard was rigid with terror. The pecking creature was working furiously on his face and had partially dislodged the blindfold, he could see from the corner of his eye, the sea was filled with black slimy creatures all seemingly trying to drag the raft under, he felt water around his face, over his body. The dark sky above him was suddenly shot through with a clear bolt of sunlight, dawn was breaking. The creatures were afraid of the light and doubled their efforts to sink the raft, Richard watched the lightening sky drift away from him as the cold, salty water covered his face filling his nostrils. Instinctively he held his breath, long seconds passed as he realised that the creatures were dropping off him to avoid the sunlight, gradually he started to drift back upwards towards the surface. The raft was waterlogged and he floated with just his face above the surface of the water, his gag had also come loose allowing him to take great gulps of air, the creatures had all disappeared.

The sun had risen quickly bathing Richard's

173

ravaged body in warmth, he managed to twist his head enough to see down his side, every square inch had a bite or peck mark, the salt water aggravated the soreness and within minutes he could see them all turning septic, they oozed. Richard's agony was complete when he saw the birds circling overhead. Birds like unnatural black gulls swooped around the raft until, as one, they plunged down onto him pecking and clawing his flesh away.

He felt himself being shaken. By waves perhaps?

"Oy! Stop a-moanin' an' wake up ya lazy bastard! We need some more firewood!" The old woman kicked him through the fabric of the tent as she went past. Richard sprang up out of the tent and glared at her, Tsuba looked up from tending to the fire,

"Are you well my friend?" He asked jovially. Richard just shrugged,

"A nightmare." He replied dully.

"Ah, dreams! The window to the soul!" Tsuba pronounced.

"Piss off!" Richard muttered and headed off to find wood.

The house in the Countryside - 2000

It was one of those sunny afternoons occasionally broken by freezing rain showers. It was during one of those occasional downpours the Sir Clive arrived at his country house. He quickly disappeared inside leaving the drunken housekeeper, Anjelica, to flounder with his bags. Kelvin Bright eventually appeared, wearing his 'country gentlemans' waxed jacket and hat, to park the car in the garage.

"You're looking a bit wet, Jelly!" He observed laughing sarcastically. He was actually quite surprised that she wasn't slumped somewhere asleep after having her lunchtime tot of brandy. She laughed with him, looking demented with her hair hanging limp like wet string down her face,

"Fuck off you fucking little ponce!" She managed to utter before he closed the car door on her. She staggered, dripping, into the house not noticing the gorgeous rainbow that had appeared across the northern sky.

Inside, she caught a glimpse of the twins curtseying and pretending to smile as they welcomed home their father, even in her alcoholic daze she had time for some sympathy for them.

"Shame. Poor little bastards. It's not their fault they're fucking mad..." She mumbled to herself while she sought out the brandy, "...Better have a little one, what with him being back in the house." She justified a large slug. And then took another.

Walther's boat, London

Susan felt the weight of Walther's pistol, it was heavy and massive in her hand. She remembered the bloody mess the bullets had made of Joan. In her minds eye she pictured Raven's face, without hesitation she raised the gun and fired, there was a satisfying click,

"It's a very good thing it wasn't loaded!" Walther vaguely chastised her.

"I'd already checked." Susan replied, without turning to him she showed a fistful of bullets that she'd removed from the gun.

"You seem quite relaxed handling that gun?" It was a leading statement.

"I am..." She answered flatly, "...Every girl should have one." She said it jokingly but Walther could tell that there was a more serious undertone to her words.

She had spent the night on the boat, in the spare berth, they had talked a great deal and made tentative plans. Walther had told her how he had been working on the engine of the old boat, making sure that it was up to the journey. He had bought provisions to last them for at least a few days and there appeared to be no reason why they could not set off on the following morning. They rose at dawn, Walther smiled as the engine started up first-time, with the sun rising behind them in the east Walther steered the boat out into the early morning traffic of the river Thames.

Susan, standing behind Walther on the small rear deck, watched as they drifted away from the mooring with a mounting sense of excitement, absent-mindedly touching the thin scars on her cheek.

Sipping black coffee as they chugged under Richmond bridge, she watched Walther's face, the lines frozen in concentration, looking every inch the Hungarian nobleman. He had confessed to her last night that he was wealthy, stinking rich even, having inherited an estate and vineyards from his father, he hoped one day to play host to her in his native country.

"If we get through this alive." She had told him.

The house in the Countryside ~ 2000

Pip and Emm had retreated from the paternal attentions of Sir Clive and hidden themselves in their

176

bedroom. They sat at their dressing table looking at each other in the mirror,

"I hate him!" One said.

"I do too!" There was a short pause while they continued to stare at each others reflections,

"We could kill him." One ventured,

"Yes. We could." One of them fetched an evil looking doll from a cupboard,

"Madame Pincer would tell us how." They stared at their customised doll with its miniature home-made knives and scissors until it advised them,

"Wait till he's been on the whisky." Another long pause,

"Then strangle him with the bell cord."

"Make it look like suicide." Another, longer pause,

"I think I hate the mistress as well!"

"And I do too!" Another pause, the longest,

"No I don't!"

"Nor I!" Then they crumbled. Hugging each other tenderly while they stared into the mirror and sobbed, hopeless and confused. And looking forward to patricide.

*

Kelvin Bright sat in the car that he'd parked in the garage, he was smoking one of the expensive cigarettes that were kept in the car's cocktail cabinet. A day-dreamer and a fool with a nasty streak,

"You want to watch out for me!..." He said to his imaginary audience, "...I'm dangerous to be around!" He boasted to himself, carelessly stubbing out the cigarette and stealing a few more for later.

177

Sir Clive stared into his half-filled crystal whisky tumbler of fine single malt scotch. Alone in his Study he was slumped on an antique leather sofa, his thoughts festering. For years he had envied Raven's immortality, he wanted it. And he had devoted almost as many years trying to find the secret.

He'd gone to considerable expense in making his cellar laboratory secure and fully equipped, installing a mini kitchen and bathroom along with the more sinister accoutrements of dentists chair and operating table. Owing to the number of 'accidental' deaths he'd had to entomb several unfortunate victims in one of the rooms, blocking off the dumb waiter and bricking up the doorway, then plastering over it as if it never existed. The only way in and out of the laboratory was through a single door, which he had reinforced with locks and bolts on both sides.

Over the years he had conducted many bizarre experiments to try to artificially reproduce Raven's mysterious gift, everything he'd tried had failed. He had bought potions and elixirs from all the corners of the world, and of course none of them had worked. He was old, getting older and more desperate. Age, alcohol, senile dementia, and the fear of death led him to contemplate greater and greater extremes.

"It's all to do with the brain..." He mused, "...There must be a way...." He tapped his temple, "...If I could only~" After downing half his glass he reached tremblingly for the telephone, dialed the ex-directory number of an old colleague who still worked for the Foreign Office, his call was answered quite promptly,

178

"Hello?"

"Giles old man! How are you?" He exchanged the customary polite nonsenses for a short time before coming to the point,

"Listen Giles, can you talk? Are you alone? You are? Good! Look, I want you to put me in contact with that Bangkok chappie, you know, the one who supplies the girls. I need a couple of lively young fillies, you know! No, don't ask why, just get me in puch with the chappie!" Sir Clive ended the conversation with a promise to 'look after' Giles if everything worked out satisfactorily.

After downing the rest of his whisky he made his way downstairs to the laboratory. He'd brought some very special instruments with him that needed to be set up carefully prior to his next experiment.

*

Raven strolled moodily around the garden, the time approaching midnight, it was quite dark; the only light coming from the house windows. She was abjectly bored, feeling both lonely and ancient. She kicked petulantly at the small flowers and shrubs as she passed them. She knew what she needed and hated herself for it. It was one of those times, which occurred, mercifully for her, only rarely, when she saw herself as a parasitic monster preying on humanity. Many times she'd argued with herself saying that she had as much right to live as anybody else, it was not her fault that she needed to kill in order to live!

Tonight her sadness was very deep, nothing seemed to please her or excite her any more. She existed merely to survive, *"I'm no good, not even to my daughter-"*

Her melancholy reverie was suddenly broken by the

179

appearance of a ghost.

A small silvery figure danced across the lawn in front of her. Raven was rarely surprised but the sight of the pale creature skipping and scampering this way and that way left her staring open-mouthed, of course she quickly realised that it was Cairo but that did not diminish the sense of surprise and wonder. The sudden thought that Cairo might be 'growing up' came as an even bigger shock. She watched, mesmerised, as her daughter drew nearer.

"Hello mother. What are you doing out here?" Cairo asked cheerfully as she drifted past like a flash of living silver moonlight. The word 'mother' hit Raven like a brick. It seemed like only yesterday that she'd given birth to the tiny girl on that tempestuous night in Egypt. And now she was... how old? She couldn't be sure.

"I've neglected you." She said simply and sadly, and then the anger came back. She hated herself and everyone else, it was time to hurt again.

Cairo couldn't possibly have heard her as she cartwheeled around the waterless fountain. She circled and reappeared breathlessly in front of Raven,

"Have you come to talk, mother?"

"Don't call me that."

"What? Call you what?"

"You know, **mother**..." She sneered at the word, adding, "...You haven't got a mother." She turned away as if to ignore her but Cairo quickly moved in front of her and daringly placed a cool palm on her mothers forehead,

"You are acting strange tonight, are you getting sick?" Neither of them had ever known a day's illness. Raven heaved an apparently bored sigh,

"Leave me alone little girl, I don't know you." She tried to be hurtful but Cairo's spirits were too high to be

180

dented that easily,

"I don't understand, what's wrong with you?" Cairo was becoming concerned, her mother appeared to be upset, it was not an emotion she'd seen her mother display before. Raven replied quietly staring into the empty fountain pool.

"Perhaps I am becoming sick, or maybe just sick of life."

"Oh mother! Don't be so silly, you'll always have me to turn to." At that remark Raven stiffened further,

"That's just it, foolish girl..." She hissed, "...I won't! You won't always be there, because one day you will die. Just like all the others. It seems like a long way off now but before I know it you will be a stiff white corpse, like all the others. Everyone dies."

Cairo paused in thought for a moment before asking,

"So how many children have you had then?" Raven paused for several seconds as if stung, then answered in a calm, distant voice,

"Not that many, not really, when you think of all the time I've had..." She remembered a child born just after the war and instantly repressed the thought, "...I can't remember much about them anyway. They all died, I know that much. One way or another, whatever I did, they all died. Just like you will."

Cairo paused again before making her reply. She spoke more softly than before as if she was unsure of herself,

"Maybe I won't. Do you remember a few days ago when Mr Underhill saved me from those horrid dogs?" Raven looked up, her eyes narrowing, and nodded while Cairo continued,

"Well, when poor Mr Underhill was suffering terribly from the pain of the dog bites... I could feel

181

something. I started to feel strong. Somewhere inside me I felt good. I can't explain it. But when I moved away from him the feeling became weaker, it almost made me want to hurt him some more. It was very hard to resist-" Cairo trailed off, unable to explain herself. Looking up she saw her mother's face lit up briefly by the light from an upstairs window, her expression a terrifying mask of pity and shame.

"It appears that the curse is complete." Raven whispered the words.

"I'm going to be like you aren't I? Aren't I mother?" Cairo moved closer, taking her mother by the arms and gently shaking her. Raven recoiled angrily like a startled cat.

"Don't touch me!..." She hissed at her daughter, "...You know I hate to be touched!" She'd thrown off Cairo's hands and pushed her away from the fountain.

In his hiding place across the lawn, beneath the slender willow branches, Mr Underhill braced himself, his fists clenched tight. He could not hear what they were saying but their movements told him that they were arguing.

Raven pointed an accusing finger at Cairo and stepped forward, with each step forward Cairo stepped backwards, they were crossing the lawn towards the willow. It was Raven's voice that Mr Underhill heard first,

"You are not going to be like me! Why do you think I've kept you away from people all your life! You're not going down that the same road to hell that I went..." Raven was becoming increasingly agitated, every thought she had making her more angry, "...Like I told you, I've had children before, and, one way or another, they all died!

YOU... they moved one step

ARE... another step

NOT... step,

LIKE... step,

ME!" Her pointing finger had turned to a fist and she seemed about to punch her daughter in the face when, with an almost inaudible rush Mr Underhill stepped out of hiding behind Cairo. Mother and daughter were both startled by his sudden huge dark presence, Cairo was first to recognise him and quickly pressed herself close against him, he felt as solid and immovable as her tree. Raven had stopped in her tracks, staring up at the huge man's grim face. She'd been in many dangerous situations before and did not feel in the least intimidated after she had recognised him. She was, however, lost for words.

"I'll talk to you tomorrow!" She rounded and headed back towards the house, calling over her shoulder,

"And I think it's past your bedtime!"

184

The house in the Countryside ~ 2000

The phone rang.

"Sir Clive?"

"Giles my dear old chap! I didn't expect to hear from you so soon!"

"Are you okay to talk?"

"Yes yes, go ahead old chap."

"Well, the goods you asked me about, you know what I mean? The Bangkok Chappie says that they're actually in stock right now, in his warehouse in London, so to speak."

"Wonderful." Sir Clive rubbed his hands together in anticipation.

"Yes. He says you can pick them up tonight if you wish."

"Yes, yes indeed! I certainly will. Where from?"

"At the Excelsior. 'Usual terms' he said."

"Yes yes yes very good. What time?"

"He suggested 11:00."

"Excellent! Thank you very much old chap, I'll look after you for this, don't you worry!"

"Thank you, but there is one more thing Sir Clive, apparently they hardly speak any English. Is that going to pose a problem?"

"Oh no, no problem at all, perfect in fact! I won't be requiring them to talk! Ha!"

Richard, near Shillingham

Richard and Tsuba set off into the woods in the early morning sunlight, Richard was amazed at how quietly

Tsuba moved through the quite dense forest. They had with them a map and compass, a bottle of water, binoculars and Tsuba's great Tanto knife on a sling inside his jacket. The plan was to survey the house and the surrounding area and try to get an idea of who was in the house at the moment, Richard had a pencil and paper inside his jacket pocket for making notes and diagrams. He felt slightly ridiculous creeping through the trees and once again asked himself why he hadn't gone to the police. He answered himself when images of Susan and Philip came into his mind, he quickly switched off, not wanting to imagine what might have happened and continued walking mechanically.

"You are very quiet my friend." Tsuba murmured softly, only a fraction louder than the rustle of the leaves, Richard still heard him quite clearly.

"I'm trying not to think." By comparison Richard's voice sounded loud and harsh, he softened it and turned to Tsuba, asking,

"Tell me again what you know about Raven, can she really be that old? Do you really think it's possible?" Tsuba's answer both confounded and greatly irritated Richard.

"But from Ebese create he can

Forms more real than living man,

Nurselings of Immortality." Richard glared at him, retorting in a harsh whisper,

"Just stuff it, okay? Stuff it sideways!..." He jabbed a finger towards Tsuba, "... If you're going to quote effing Shakespeare every time I ask you a straight question then I'd rather we didn't talk at all!"

Tsuba glanced at Richard with amusement glinting in his eyes,

"Shakespeare?..." He laughed gently, "...I think not

186

my friend..." He laughed a little further and stepped away before uttering,

'Dress'd in a little brief authority

Most ignorant of what he's most assur'd'. That, my friend, was Shakespeare."

They didn't talk again for some time.

Walther's boat

"So tell me some more about your inheritance." Susan asked Walther. They had moored for a while, Walther had pinpointed their position as,

"Somewhere between Chertsey and Staines." and they were having a light lunch.

He finished his sandwich and, while still chewing, began rummaging inside a drawer,

"Here it is." He produced a map of Hungary, unfolding it carefully he laid it on the table in front of Susan, he sat across from her and looked at it upside down.

"See here." He pointed to the city of Pecs in the south-west of the country.

"My home is a few kilometres to the south-east of the city, roughly half-way between Pecs and the Danube. It is a beautiful land that yields excellent grapes, our wines are very good." She could tell that he was proud of his homeland, looking into his face she could see a trace of wistfulness, as if he was a little homesick. It was another conversation that rapidly dried up.

After a little while Susan cleared up the lunch things saying,

"I think we'd better get moving again, don't you?" Walther agreed and got the engine going.

The house in the Countryside ~ 2000

Raven thought about Cairo. About Cairo's father. And wept. No sound, not even a shudder as they spilled down her face, the tears of regret.

She thought of the time she had spent with Tsuba, how the years had slipped by, how she had become a little tired of his simple honesty when she met Erik. The wiry blond archaeologist with a fondness for drink and sex. The two men could not have been more opposite. She loved them both, and enjoyed herself. But it could not last, and the ultimatums were made. She would not choose between them and so chose neither, running away in the night. Pregnant.

It was Erik who found her, months later in the city of Cairo.

"It's yours." She had said, indicating her bump. He stayed close to her from then, babbling about the future. And when the baby was born thrilling at his little girl's black hair and how much she looked like her mother. As ever, love was blind.

*

Richard stopped at Tsuba's urgent whisper,

"We are almost there." Tsuba had stopped walking, and turning his head from right to left and back again, he studied the forest. Richard wanted to ask him *"How do you know that?"* but he thought better of it, instead he also stared at the forest in the hope of getting some idea of what Tsuba was doing, he saw nothing.

188

"We should circle around that way." Tsuba pointed towards higher ground barely visible through the gaps between the trees and away to their left.

"And now my friend..." He stopped Richard with a palm on his chest, "...We need to be very quiet and remain unseen! Yes?" Richard understood, he was being gently chastised, he realised that it was no time to be petty or churlish.

"Yes..." He replied simply, "...I'll do my best... lead on MacDuff!" Tsuba smiled at Richard's reply, he was relieved,

"Good! Then let us enter the fray!" He turned and vanished into the thicker undergrowth.

"Don't wait for me..." Richard whispered as he dived in behind him, "...I'll keep up."

A short while later they got their first glimpse of the old mansion house, nestled half-way down the gently sloping fields dropping down to the river in the distance.

"That must be the Thames." Richard mused, Tsuba nodded, he was busily scanning in all different directions, looking for a better spot to view the house and a safe way to approach it, after a few minutes careful scrutiny he pointed out a direction,

"Follow me, and stay very low." They moved downwards from the higher ground taking care to always have trees and bushes between themselves and the house, at last Tsuba raised his hand again and they stopped,

"I think that this is about the best we will get." He said, handing the binoculars over to Richard. He immediately put them up and was surprised by the excellent view they had of the house. He was looking at the front and one side of it, the sun was behind them lighting up the house in excellent relief. They surveyed the buildings, drawing sketches, until late afternoon, seeing no one, but hearing the sounds of shotgun fire and dogs barking.

On the way back to camp Richard was edgy,

"Correct me if I'm wrong, and no doubt you will, but wasn't that a complete waste of time?" Tsuba stopped and looked at Richard, he was clearly exasperated, he replied in a crisp sharp manner,

"Quite the contrary, we have learned a great deal."

"Huh? Like what for instance?" Richard was incredulous while Tsuba related in infuriated tones,

"The house has few occupants and even fewer daily visitors. There are dogs; I counted two, didn't you? They have a shotgun and very likely other weapons besides. We know where to approach the house without being seen, and we know approximately how many rooms are on each floor. In my opinion we should watch for one more day and then plan our attack for the following dawn..." Tsuba released a sigh and regained his normal placid veneer, "... Can I take it that you agree?"

Richard felt stupid and useless, angry with himself he wanted to say something sarcastic, he desperately tried to think of some clever riposte,

"Yeah sure." He managed to say.

Later that evening after their evening meal, the odd threesome sat around the camp fire, conversation was limited.

"So how come you know so much about Shakespeare and stuff if you grew up in the Cambodian war, I thought Pol Pot was against that sort of thing?" Tsuba had been whittling with his knife, he stopped for a moment and thought, then began again before answering Richard,

"I was born in Japan. As I told you before..." He turned his face to the sky, "...And I was, erm, dissatisfied

190

with the comfortable life I had. I…" He laughed, "…I ran away to sea. Spent a couple of years drifting the South China Seas until I ended up in Cambodia…" His face darkened, "…So much happened there. And I have travelled far since then…" He made a visible effort to lighten the mood, "…But to answer your question…" He waved towards the miserable old woman, "…Francesca here…" She was oblivious, "…Used to be an actress, a real trouper, she has performed much of Shakespeare's work, the plays are on the bus. They make good reading." Richard was a little interested,

"So she's a failed actress." He pointed out unkindly.

"That depends on your definition of failure. In Francesca's case she had throat cancer, she was lucky they said, they managed to save her life, unfortunately they couldn't save her voice. I'm sure even you understand that a Shakespearean actress needs a powerful voice." Tsuba fell quiet and continued his whittling.

The old woman spat on the ground and staggered over to the bus. Richard felt very small in a very big world, he rose,

"I'll go and see if I can find enough wood to last through the night." Tsuba simply nodded in reply, his eyes fixed on the small dancing flames, his mind half a world away as he remembered the time Raven had saved his life. The oath that he'd made to protect her, and the way she had left him.

And the years he had spent at first trying to forget her, and then trying to find her, *"And now I have a man in my camp who wants to kill you. That will not happen, I will help him to find you, yes, but I will not let harm come to you…"* Tsuba pondered the impossible situation he found himself in and as usual found a little Shakespeare to help him, *"...Our wills and fates do so contrary run."*

*

"Bright! **Bright!** Bring the Rolls round to the front of the house..." Sir Clive bellowed out his orders, "...You're driving me to the City."

"What? Right now?" Kelvin Bright was obviously put-out by the sudden order.

"Yes now damn it! And mind your damned impudence! Or you won't be driving for me much longer!"

"Yes Sir!" Bright sparked up. Muttering "Fat old bastard." under his breath as he went.

"Anjelica! Confound it woman where are you?" Anjelica appeared, red faced and leaning against the door frame,

"Did you call me sir?" She barely managed to utter.

"Good heavens woman! Are you drunk?"

"Oh good lord no sir! Just a little woozy, that's all, been working hard all morning." She hiccuped.

"I want one of the spare rooms ready for when I get back, make it the double one next to mine, I'll have a couple of young ladies to entertain. Are you listening to me woman!?"

The car pulled up outside, Kelvin impertinently sounding the horn.

"We'll be back in the early hours, do not disappoint me Anjelica!" He warned her.

"No Sir! I won't Sir! You can always rely on me sir!" The thought of him entertaining two young ladies sent her fleeing to the bathroom to vomit.

*

192

Walther studied the Ordnance Survey Map with a microscope; he had moored the boat to a muddy bank a few minutes earlier and darkness had begun to fall. Susan had gone on deck for a look around and was surprised when he immediately called her back in.

"Why?" She had asked.

"I'm not sure yet." He peered through binoculars out through the cabin window at a house half way up the gently sloping valley.

"I think that's it." He said.

"What? The house? Do you mean we've found it already?" Susan was incredulous.

"Yes, it was easier than I'd thought, there it is." They both fell silent for a moment, Susan chewed her lip like she used to when she was nervous. Walther resumed his study of the map,

"Now we must carefully consider our next move."

Raven, on the prowl, High Wycombe

Raven had found him drinking in a bar in High Wycombe. She chatted to him, established that he was staying alone in his 'second home',

"I'm in the jewellery business..." It sounded like a boast, "...Diamonds and such..." It was, "...Are a girls best friend the saying goes." She smiled at his lack of charm and let him continue,

"The wife n kids are at home in leafy Leamington Spa, much easier to commute into town from here though, Monday to Thursday you'll always find me in my little pad..." He sniggered, "...If you ever want to drop by~" She interrupted him,

193

"Why not now?..." She made the suggestion very suggestive, "...I'd love to see your little pad." They finished their drinks and walked the short distance to his flat, an uninspiring first floor conversion, he continued to do most of the talking,

"Doesn't look much on the outside, I'll grant you..." He put the key in the door, "...But don't judge a book by its cover eh? Wait till you see what I've done with the place." He showed her in, took her jacket, hung it in the hallway next to his own and led her into the living room. She was, slightly impressed, and said so,

"I like what you've done." He had recreated the likeness of a 'gentleman's study', with comfortable leather chairs, bookcases, a drinks cabinet and the long wall covered with pictures.

The self-satisfied gentleman gestured proudly towards his collection of fine art prints, his voice loud and pompous,

"Of course they're not the originals..." He laughed absurdly, "...They're all in museums..." This was apparently humorous, so Raven obliged him with a smile, "...But these are the finest prints money can buy..." He was very pleased with himself and his red cheeks bloomed in evidence, "...And what I've spent on the frames!" Raven looked at them, her inner fury barely held at bay.

He turned to fix drinks.

She joined him smiled, and offered,

"I make a very good Manhattan, or so I've been told." He nodded, not knowing if he had the ingredients,

"Go ahead, by all means, use whatever~"

"I'll need the kitchen..." She strolled across the room holding a bottle of bourbon, "...Through here?..." She pointed to a likely door, "...Why don't you put on something

194

more comfortable while I make drinks?" He nodded again, pointed to another door,

"Back in a jiffy!" He disappeared, Raven entered the kitchen. The cooker appeared unused, but there was a fine knife rack next to it, she selected the best for the job and returned to the living room. In seconds she had crushed a little pill into his glass and added the bourbon. He returned eager and expectant, she pressed the glass into his hand,

"You don't have the ingredients..." Raised it to his lips, "...I prefer it neat anyway..." Raised hers and chinked, "...Down the hatch..." She downed hers in one, he did the same. Game over.

Raven slipped away from the corpse, cleaned the knife and then showered, she always believed in making a quick getaway for if she had any fear at all, it was of capture, her memories of medieval incarceration too vivid for her to forget.

She dressed looking at the wall gallery, pride of place went to Rubens' The Mantuan circle of friends', it caused her to pause,

"Friends..." She sneered at the concept, "...I never met anyone who didn't want something in return for their so-called friendship..." She gazed up at the Baroque masterpiece hanging before her, "...They always have a reason why they want to be your friend, be it for sex, or for your money or for your influence..." The painting remained unmoved by her bitter rant, "...Or they want you simply so that no one else can have you..." She turned away from the painting, "...Friends are just people who haven't betrayed you yet..." The magnificent painting looked down at her, she recalled the jewelers words,

"Diamonds are a girl's best friend" And disagreed,

"Not so, jeweler..." She turned to face his bloody corpse, "...In this world, this life..." She made for the door, "...Daggers are a girls best friend."

Chapter 6
"...could you forgive, my deadly desire?"

Sir Clive at The Excelsior 10:30 P.M.

"Wait for me at the bar." Bright had been told. It was a Strip club, owned and run by Asians, they specialised in Asian girls.

Sir Clive took a seat at a table near the front, shortly after seating himself he was approached by a waitress who led him away to a table on the far side of the club. Through the dim light and smoke Bright could barely see him.

Sir Clive had been seated at a large oblong table with the Bangkok Chappie facing him. Behind him at the next table sat two well-dressed burly men, his bodyguards, behind the Bangkok Chappie sat two Asian girls, he could not quite see them properly.

"Greetings Sir Clive, it is good to see you again." The Bangkok Chappie spoke with a strong accent.

"Likewise I'm sure." Sir Clive was arrogant, he 'didn't have time' for colonial upstarts.

It was obvious that there was to be no more small talk. The Bangkok Chappie grinned showing his gold teeth as he spoke,

"I believe we agreed on the usual terms? Plus insurance."

"What!? What the bloody hell is insurance!" Sir Clive was indignant, the Bangkok Chappie raised his hands in placation,

"Let me explain..." He said coldly, Sir Clive held his tongue, "...obtaining girls for the enjoyment of the western world is easy, fathers are always ready to offload their expensive daughters..." He smiled and lit up a black cigarette, "...However, selling them on again is not so easy. In fact, your prudish, hypocritical governments are making it increasingly difficult for me to trade effectively."

"That's **your** problem!" Sir Clive interrupted, and annoyance showed plain on The Bangkok Chappie's face.

"Do not interrupt me! Please." He stared ferociously at Sir Clive who became uncomfortably aware of the two henchmen sat behind him. He looked nervously towards the bar from where Bright should have been watching, but the shifty chauffeur had his eyes trained firmly on the strippers.

"As I was saying." Sir Clive turned back to face the Bangkok Chappie.

"Yes, I'm sorry, please carry on my good man." A smile returned to the Asian's face.

"You will give me two cheques for £10,000 each, these are not for me, they are for the families of the girls, for this money they will be silent. For this money they will even forget that they had these daughters. I will see to it. This is your insurance." Sir Clive had to interrupt,

"Cheques can be traced." With a dismissive gesture the Bangkok Chappie silenced him before he could object any further,

"Yes, of course they can. That is my insurance. My services have been rendered at the usual terms to you, but if I am questioned about these girls at some future time I will not know if they even existed, your cheques will show only that you bought the girls yourself direct from their families."

There was a brief silence between the two men, but the Bangkok Chappie had no patience for the pompous English buffoon, he rasped out heatedly,

"Do you wish to own these lovely girls or not? I have other customers you know." He leaned to one side, allowing Sir Clive a better view of the girls, he couldn't help but look. They were young, they were tiny, and they were pretty. But he thought about their brains and dreamed of his own immortality. The Bangkok Chappie encouraged him further,

"They will be yours and yours alone, to do with as you wish. Whatever you want will be their delight" Of course the Chappie had no idea what Sir Clive's real intentions were, he presumed they were for his sexual gratification, he stubbed out his cigarette and took a sip of his drink, confident that the transaction would soon be completed.

Sir Clive was sweating, again he looked across at Bright who was still ogling the strippers. The Bangkok Chappie continued talking,

"See the one on the left, her name is Mai, she is a virgin. The girl on the right, her name is Rita, she has flawless skin. As I said, I do have other customers you know."

Sir Clive reached for his cheque book.

The house in the Countryside - 2000

Early the next morning Richard and Tsuba again took up position in the woods to watch over the house. Richard having vowed to himself that he would try to be more useful and less childish.

They immediately notice the Rolls-Royce parked in front of the house. Richard wondered if it was the car that he'd been transported in. It made him think of the twins and he wondered, bizarrely, if they were okay. He speculated that it might be Sir Clive who arrived in the night, he remembered that the twins had spoken of him once or twice.

A short while later they saw a youngish man drive the car around the house onto the blind side, they presumed there was a garage, Richard guessed that the man was Kelvin Bright, the chauffeur, whom Cairo had mentioned had the shotgun and the dogs. Tsuba was pleased with the extra information.

There was very little activity during the rest of the morning, and at some point Richard gazed around the surrounding countryside until he saw that a houseboat had moored on the nearside riverbank. He did a double take and then quick as a flash he grabbed the binoculars from Tsuba and trained them on the boat,

"It can't be! I don't believe it, I know that boat!" Tsuba had to grab him and pull him back down into hiding,

"Sit back down you crazy fool! What have you seen?"

"That's Walther's boat. You remember, the guy that got us involved in all this! He's here!"

"How can you be so sure? They make many boats to the same specification." Tsuba reasoned that it was unlikely to be the same boat, but Richard wasn't having it,

"Oh it's his boat all right, believe me, there won't be another one like that. Anyway, we have to find out." Richard was right this time and he knew it, Tsuba knew it too,

"Yes, my friend... you are right. We do need to know. If your friend Walther is on that boat, then I think we can safely assume his mission is the same as ours."

"Great, let's go then!" Richard eagerly packed up their things, then Tsuba led the way in a great loop around the house always making sure they were hidden from sight. It was nearly half an hour later when they arrived at the boat. They hid for a while and watched, then decided that one of them should approach the boat alone.

"I'll do it, you cover me." Richard announced in a tone that suggested no compromise.

"Yes." Tsuba agreed without comment and with no further pause Richard broke cover and approached the boat from the rear. All was quiet except for the birds and the ripples, carefully Richard stepped on to the little deck at the rear of the boat causing it to rock gently. Inside Susan and Walther noticed instantly and jumped into action in case it was anyone from the house. Susan quickly loaded the gun while Walther called out to the stranger on deck,

"Who's there!?"

"I'm looking for Walther!" Came Richard's muffled reply, Susan found the voice disconcertingly familiar but couldn't quite place it.

"What do you want?" Walther demanded. There was a tiny pause before Richard replied,

"I'm a friend of his, I just happened to be passing by when I saw his boat!" Richard knew as soon as he'd said it that he sounded ridiculous, *"So what?"* he said to himself, then he shouted through the door again,

"His name is Walther. Is he in there?" Susan felt a cold shiver run down her spine, she moved forward and clutched Walther's sleeve, he turned, she was pale and seemed frightened,

"What is it?" He asked. She shook her head and frowned,

"It's his voice..." She said quavering, ...He sounds just like Richard!" Walther looked doubtful and gently pushed

201

her behind himself, carefully he opened the cabin door making sure to leave the chain on, and peering through the crack he saw a tall, gaunt, unshaven man who looked vaguely like Richard.

"Walther! It's me! What's wrong don't you recognise me?!" Susan had heard enough, pushing Walther aside she tore open the cabin door, for a second she paused, taking all of him in. He was taller, *"Not possible"* He was much thinner, *"Steak and chips"* And he was unshaven and very dirty, *"You need a shower!"*

"Richard!" She had no words appropriate. He looked at her, and his face ran through as many expressions as possible in three seconds. Shock, shame, fear, relief, and finally joy. The sudden rush of emotions overwhelmed him, his legs gave way and he sank to his knees and cried, swaying there on his own on the deck he cried. Susan watched him, powerless to touch him after all she'd been through.

Walther quietly stepped off the boat and walked away for a few paces to give them some privacy. Tsuba watched impassively from the shelter of the bushes.

"I thought you were dead."

"I very nearly was! I thought you were dead too."

"You look like shit."

"You look great!" Susan knelt down in front of Richard, they wrapped arms around each other and held tight.

*

Breakfast time was at 9.00am whenever Sir Clive was at home. He sat at the head of a large oval table, this time flanked on his right side by the two Asian girls Rita

202

and Mai, on his left were Pip and Emm. Raven never ate breakfast, Franco could not stand to be in the same room as Sir Clive and nobody ever knew where Cairo was at any given time so the table was only half occupied.

The girls, Rita and Mai, were dressed like whores, all lipstick and cheap jewellery. Pip and Emm had on their 'breakfast' dresses, neatly ironed Gingham check. None spoke except Sir Clive, apart from the occasional giggle from Rita whenever Anjelica appeared with another tray of food, the ordeal lasted for about forty minutes before Pip and Emm could excuse themselves. They hurried upstairs to their room and locked the door behind them.

*

Cairo sat, tense and uneasy on her bed, legs crossed, the forehead above her dark eyes furrowed by a frown. She always felt that way when Sir Clive was at home but this time it was worse. Recent events had changed everything, her mind was in constant turmoil. She was worried about her mother but she was in even more consternation about her own situation. She constantly thought about Richard, *"Where was he?..."* She pursed her neat lips, *"...Will he really come back like he promised?"* She imagined leaving the house, running away into the woods like Richard had done. She desperately wanted to talk to somebody, Mr Underhill was nice but not someone she could confide her innermost thoughts to.

Then there was Button, she had always told him everything, but since that night with Richard she had left him neglected under the bed. She needed him again, but not like before, not under the bed with twilight whisperings, she needed him out in the daylight - in the

203

real world!

Slowly and a little nervously she reached under the bed, he was still there where she had left him, gently she pulled him out. She could not remember the last time she had seen him in daylight. He gave her quite a shock. The old teddy was shapeless and filthy, and worst of all he was lifeless. He was dead to her. With gut-crunching sadness she held him close for several minutes, no idea what to do, finally, with great courage, she crossed her room and placed him on a shelf with many of the other relics of her childhood.

Sitting on the floor beneath her window, unable to cry, for the first time in her solitary life she felt completely alone.

*

Raven had been out riding again, Franco approached her on her way back to the house while nobody was in earshot,

"Mistress..." He had taken the opportunity to speak candidly to her, "...We should quit this place, we should leave while we still can!"

"Why?" She demanded simply as they approached the house. Franco stepped in front of her, forcing her to stop. It was a liberty he had seldom taken recently, she flared up instantly, raising her arms to push him out of the way, Franco would not be moved, he gripped her arms tightly and forced them down to her sides. She was livid,

"That's the second time I've been manhandled in the last twelve hours..." She hissed menacingly, "...Get away from me!" She screamed at him and punched him hard in the face. He took the blow and stood like a rock. She hit

204

him again, splitting his lip.

"Please listen." His eyes pleaded. His face told her that she could do anything to him but that he absolutely would not move until he'd been heard. She regretted hitting him.

"Very well Franco, I will listen, but not out here. I'm hot and sweaty, come with me to my room. I want to find out what's gotten in to you!" She marched ahead of him adding,

"And I warn you! Don't ever lay hands on me like that again!" She of course had to have the last word.

Upstairs in her rooms, Franco waited while she showered. She had stripped shamelessly in front of him, *"Was it just a tease? Or?~"* He wondered. He had turned his back quickly enough anyway, not wishing to be reminded of something he had once had but could never have again.

Raven strolled into the room wearing a short, Japanese style, dressing gown,

"Now I feel much better!" Franco stood at the window waiting patiently as always. She spoke to his back,

"I'm sorry I hit you, come here let me have a look at that lip." They moved together at the centre of the room, she tenderly pulled down his lip to inspect the damage,

"Hmm, you've had worse, many times, I think you'll live! Now tell me why we should leave here so urgently." Franco looked pained,

"It will be difficult to explain, Mistress. Most of my reasons are not concrete, just intuition."

"I trust your intuition, you know that." She flopped down on to her bed as she spoke, Franco had remained standing, pacing back and forth.

"Firstly, Mistress, I know you are unhappy here. You

205

have been for some time. Cairo is also deeply unhappy, although she probably doesn't know the full extent of it, she needs to be with other people her own age. It is not healthy for her here. But there is more to it than that, I'm afraid of what that madman in the cellar..." He paused, pointing downwards for emphasis, "...And his experiments might bring. He could bring ruin to us all..." He waited for a moment, then continued as if he'd at last come to the point, "...And I'm also afraid of Von Vohburg and his friends, somehow I feel certain that they will come here to destroy you..." He stared at the carpet, adding, "...And I'm so afraid that this time I may not be able to stop them, I am..." He clearly hated to say it, "...Getting old." With a nod Raven encouraged him to continue,

"You must not rely on that whelp, Bright, to help you, he is..." Franco struggled for the words and settled for, "...A no-good son-of-a-bitch!..." Raven stifled a snort as he continued, "...Let us go back to the continent, Spain perhaps? There I might be able to find someone to replace me, someone who would be devoted to you." He trailed off not knowing if she'd been listening or not, feeling ashamed for admitting his fear and weakness. But Raven had been listening carefully, and she saw the sense in his words, she would be sad to lose him but had always known it would happen some day. She replied almost tenderly,

"Thank you dear Franco, my world will be an emptier place without you, I hope you always remember that..." She flashed a smile that could melt lead, "...And yes I agree with you, we shall leave this place, and, now that the decision is made, the sooner the better. Go find Cairo, tell her we are leaving tomorrow. Tell her to pack a bag, just one mind! Well go on, don't just stand there grinning, hurry up you old grizzly bear!"

"Yes Mistress. And thank you!" Franco fled the room feeling taller and stronger than he had for a long time.

"And as for me..." Raven spoke to herself in her empty bedroom, "...My bag was never unpacked."

The house in the Countryside ~ 2000

Mai was left watching television in the guest room while Sir Clive took Rita down to the laboratory. At the sight of the white tiled walls and steel furniture Rita became quite nervous, Sir Clive calmed her down with a smile and a drink that contained a heavy sedative. She was shortly reclining on Sir Clive's purpose made adjustable divan. He had been lusting for her since he'd bought her the previous evening and lost no time in tearing off her clothes, the Bangkok Chappie had not lied, her skin was flawless and her tiny body exquisite. He abused it in every way he could imagine until he was satisfied. And then eventually the experiment could begin.

Rita hardly knew what was happening to her, she suffered it all in a dream-like, no, a nightmare-like trance.

"It's all to do with the brain." Sir Clive's own mind was way past the point of no return, he was clinically insane, completely barking mad. He had lost all track of time and it was early evening before the experiment began, on a large flip chart he'd written down his latest demented theory in bold block-capitals:

IMMORTALITY CAN BE ACHIEVED BY THE REGULAR INGESTION Of LIVING HUMAN BRAIN MATTER, THIS WOULD ARREST, AND LIKELY REVERSE, THE NORMAL AGEING PROCESS

The crackpot theory made no mention of how or why it would achieve this, his unbalanced mind simply presumed it would work.

He moved the sedated Rita onto the operating table securing her feet, arms and middle with straps to prevent her moving, then he tilted the whole table at a 45 degree angle with her feet nearly touching the floor, that left her head at a convenient height for him to work on.

Shaving her head and letting her long silky black hair fall to the floor aroused the lust in him once again, forcing him to postpone the experiment for another few minutes more. It was the need to use the toilet that finally alerted Sir Clive to the passage of time, having been in the laboratory for several hours.

Eventually he realised that he was exhausted, hungry and having difficulty in focusing his eyes. And so it was with reluctance that he concluded the experiment would not be able to continue until the next morning.

He released the girl from the operating table and lifted her back on to the divan, covering her with a sheet. Should she wake up before morning there was a little toilet in the laboratory that she could use, so without even slight pangs of conscience he locked her in there for the night.

On his way upstairs he called in to the kitchen ordering the cook to send some food up to his room, he was tired and needed an early night. When he got up to his suite, Mai, his other little purchase, was still watching television, she smiled nervously and looked beyond him to see if Rita was there, Sir Clive spoke to her but she obviously didn't understand many words of English.

"We're going to have something to eat and drink, then I'm going to have your virginity. Okay?" She recognised the word 'Okay' and smiled, Sir Clive smiled too.

*

Franco passed the twins' bedroom door feeling a pang of sympathy for them, but he knew that as long as Sir Clive was alive they would, at least, be sheltered. He had been looking for Cairo and was surprised to find her in her bedroom, sat on the floor; usually her bedroom was the last place you would expect to find her. She was wearing a man's t-shirt that was much too large for her, her legs and feet were bare.

"Hello Franco." She didn't sound as chirpy as usual. He smiled at her,

"Your mother sent me to find you, I have a message."

"Oh?" She tried to sound uninterested. Franco could barely keep the emotion out of his voice,

"You are to pack a bag. We are leaving tomorrow." He waited for a reaction. She jumped to her feet, full of questions,

"Leaving!? Leaving where? Leaving here?" She stood before him, tiny and incredulous.

"Yes. We're finally going to quit this stinking zoo of a house." He looked around at the ceiling and the walls as if he despised them, forgetting that it was the only home that Cairo had ever known. She stood in front of him trying to absorb the concept of leaving.

"Pack a bag? What do I put in it? Where are we going? **Who** is going?" Franco put a gentle arm on her shoulder and led her across the room to her bed; they sat down together side by side, a huge caring man, a small bundle of youth,

"Your mother, myself and you will be leaving this house tomorrow. We are going over the sea to the continent, you will love it. There's so much to see – and that includes the 'sea' itself. Cairo we're going to travel, to show you the world!"

She was enthralled, utterly. All her recent dreams were going to come true after all! She jumped up and danced around the room, kicking up the dust of years, clapping her hands and laughing like a happy little girl,

"Where is mother? I must see her now!"

"I believe she is in her bedroom." He called out as she skipped out of her room, along the landing, down a short flight of stairs and knocked on Raven's bedroom door.

"Mother? Are you there?" She called out cheerfully remembering that she had only been inside that room a handful of times in her entire life.

"Come in." Cairo entered the opulently decorated boudoir in hushed excitement.

Raven was seated at an ornately carved bureau, writing in a book. She had large elegant handwriting.

"Mother I'm so excited! We're going away!" Cairo fizzed. Raven put down her pen with a mock frown,

"I hope you're not going to keep calling me mother everywhere we go! Or else I might have to leave you behind!" Raven half-joked and Cairo's enthusiasm was undiminished, catching sight of the journal in front of Raven,

"I didn't know you kept a diary!?" She moved to pick it up but Raven quickly closed it and slid it into a drawer.

"Yes, well actually I've kept several, I only write occasional entries, the important things. Things that I might actually want to remember some day." Cairo wasn't at that moment very interested.

"What time are we leaving?" She asked, bobbing up and down on the spot.

"As soon as we're ready. We will take the white car, the convertible, so much more stylish and comfortable in the hotter countries. I haven't told Sir Clive yet, I haven't seen him actually." Cairo's face darkened at the mention of him,

"I think he's in his so-called laboratory. He gives me the horrors you know." She confessed.

"Does he?" Raven seemed a little surprised.

"Yes. And he's taken another girl down there! Poor thing." Cairo shuddered involuntarily. Raven frowned in thought and turned away.

"That explains it then." She said quietly, more to herself than Cairo.

"Explains what?" Cairo had overheard her.

"Oh nothing. Just a feeling I had earlier."

"What? You felt it too?" Mother and daughter looked at each other closely, not speaking. Eventually Raven changed the subject back to their forthcoming travel.

"You're allowed one bag and that's all, when we travel; we travel light!" She'd risen from her chair and flung open a wardrobe door, Cairo stepped up beside her asking,

"But what should I take? I haven't-" Raven interrupted her,

"Just a few of your favourite clothes and things, I've

211

got the passports (courtesy of Sir Clive's friends at the Foreign Office) and we've got all the money we need, so simply pack what you like."

Cairo looked around her mother's bedroom, it was crammed with things, the relics of her long life.

"Won't you miss all of these things?" She asked. Raven shrugged as if she didn't care,

"No, not really, I've lost a hundred times as much before, many times in fact. Possessions don't really mean that much at my age." She laughed. Without thinking Cairo moved forward and hugged her mother. At first Raven stiffened, then she softened and surprised herself by hugging her daughter tightly.

*

The following morning several things happened all at once. Sir Clive cancelled the breakfast ritual in favour of an early visit to the Lab. Raven took out one of the horses for an early gallop while Franco loaded the car with their bags, and Walther decided to take a breath of fresh air. He stood on the deck of his boat sipping a morning coffee. Tsuba was due back soon, he had left Richard with Susan and returned to the old woman and the bus alone, saying cryptically as usual,

"A man will not become wise if he accepts everything without question." Richard took a load of no notice and continued to hug his wife.

Walther had given up his sleeping cabin for them, very little had been said the previous evening but they had all agreed with Richard's suggestion that they carry out the attack the next morning as he and Tsuba had already planned.

212

*

Down in the laboratory Sir Clive found Rita sitting on the edge of the divan, she looked terrified and her eyes were swollen with many hours of crying.

"There, there my dear, no need to cry, it will all be over soon." She looked at him uncomprehendingly, accusingly clutching handfuls of her shaven-off hair. Sir Clive calmly filled a hypodermic with sedative, she sat unresisting as he jabbed it into her arm, big warm tears rolling down her face. Merciful oblivion followed shortly. Sir Clive laid her on the operating table, donned a surgeon's gown and with his pathologist's shiny tools set about removing the top of her skull.

"It's all to do with the brain." He repeated softly to himself like a mantra.

*

Instead of her usual canter across the fields Raven decided to take the horse down to the river, it was another bright clear morning with spring flowers and blossoms decorating the riverbank. She felt good, she was looking forward to leaving the house, and England altogether, which was becoming such a restrictive society. She rode with her mind elsewhere, imagining herself on the streets of Pamplona once again, her recent melancholia vanished.

When she saw the houseboat she thought nothing of it. When she saw the man standing on the deck she nearly fell off her horse.

"Von Vohberg!" She hissed his name followed by a sharp intake of breath. She reined in the horse and trotted

213

slowly forward, a cryptic smile gradually spreading across her face. On the deck the man turned casually at the sound of the horse approaching, first he admired the animal then glanced at the rider with a polite smile on his face. His smile quickly faded as he recognised her, even though it was the first time he'd seen her in the flesh there could be no mistaking her. She brought her horse to a stop beside the boat, patted its neck gently then fixed Walther with a Medusa-like glare,

"You look like your father..." She leaned forward, "...Cat got your tongue?" She purred slowly. Walther found himself unable to reply, awestruck by her presence, his mouth felt dry and he coughed, spilling some of his coffee. Suddenly she spurred the horse and galloped away towards the house, with her spell broken Walther dashed down into the cabin yelling for Richard and Susan to get up,

"She's seen us! She's been here!" He shouted through their cabin door. In a matter of seconds the three of them were standing on the river bank, Susan toting the gun.

"Where's Tsuba? Isn't he here yet?" Richard took charge.

"We can't afford to wait for him, he'll have to catch us up, we've either got to attack now or wait to be attacked ourselves, we have to take the initiative!"

"I agree!" Susan said. Walther hesitated for only a second,

"Yes. I have to agree also, let us move swiftly for already we have lost the element of surprise!"

Raven galloped back to the house, ignoring the stables she rode around to the front where Franco was cramming their luggage into the long white convertible. She called to him as she approached along the gravel

214

drive, her eyes sparkling,

"It seems that your intuition was right yet again!..."
She jumped from the horse a second before it had stopped,
"...Von Vohberg is here! On a houseboat, and I'll wager he's
not alone!" She called over her shoulder as she ran into the
house,

"Where's Bright?!" Franco dropped the rest of the
luggage and followed her, he loved to see her so vibrant, so
full of energy. She caught up with Bright in the kitchen
having his breakfast,

"Bright! Get your shotgun and plenty of rounds!
There are trespassers down by the river, I want you to see
them off, shoot them if necessary!" The man's jaw dropped
and he choked on a mouthful, looking doubtful. Raven
rounded on him like a Furie, fixing him with her
spellbinding gaze, her eyes holding him, she had to
motivate him,

"Why do you think I've kept you here? This is your
moment Kelvin Bright, the moment you've been waiting
for, the chance to show the world what kind of a man you
really are! It's your high noon, just DO IT RAMBO!" She
chased him from the room, then turned,

"And you! She raised a forefinger towards Fidelma,

"You heard nothing!" Raven issued the warning with
a grimace that intimated dire consequences, Fidelma
looked down and began to gather Kelvin's breakfast
things,

"To be sure, t'was nothin' to hear." She replied as she
carted everything over to the sink.

*

After checking the gun and grabbing all the spare

215

cartridges, Richard, Susan and Walther immediately left for the house, trusting that Tsuba would follow. They headed along the edge of the woods until they found a path. Kelvin Bright, looking every bit the weekend soldier in his flak jacket and peaked G.I.'s cap, met them just beyond the edge of the garden. His last two dogs, already worked up into a frenzy, were let loose,

"Terminate!" He roared out the familiar order.

*

Sir Clive carefully rinsed Rita's brain under the running tap, her body on the operating table no longer of interest to him,

"Now we shall see." He placed it on a steel tray and reached for a long scalpel.

*

"Whoa!" Richard, at the head of the three, was first to see the dogs and ducked behind a large thorn bush. The two dogs, foaming and snarling, lurched straight past him, launching themselves at Susan and Walther.

Susan, second in the file, raised her gun. Walther, with remarkable speed, tore off his jacket and began to wrap it around his left arm.

In a matter of seconds the leading dog leapt howling at Susan, she managed to get one shot off before it crashed into her chest, its jaws snapping shut an inch from her throat as she was knocked backwards to the ground.

A second later the other dog tore into Walther, fastening its powerful jaws around his wrapped arm, the animals strength was incredible, throwing its head from

216

side to side until Walther's arm was wrenched from its socket, the beast's fangs biting deeper and deeper into his arm.

Susan's single shot had been a good one, it had killed the beast as it fell upon her, but its dead weight brought her down sending the gun spinning away as she banged her head on the ground. Dizzily, she groped around for the gun to help Walther. Kelvin appeared moments later, yelling,

"Fucking bitch! You killed him you fuckin' little bitch!" His shotgun was shouldered ready to fire at her. Richard leapt out,

"Hey!" He cried out to distract Kelvin who swivelled with well-practiced ease and fired at Richard. He couldn't miss.

At the same moment as Kelvin swivelled, Tsuba leapt from the bushes and rushed upon him, with his left hand he pushed the shotgun barrel aside as it went off, Richard felt the heat, and his eyes were stung by the flash but he caught only a few stray pellets in his left shoulder.

Tsuba's right hand glittered as it moved upwards in a wide slash, catching Kelvin in the neck. The shimmering blade didn't stop and Richard watched wide-eyed as Kelvin's head flew spinning high into the air, still mouthing breathless obscenities.

Another gunshot, Richard turned to the sound and saw Susan standing over the body of the other dog, Walther lay on the ground groaning, his left arm at an odd angle to his body.

Kelvin's head, GI cap still intact, fell to the ground with a thump at Richards feet, whilst his upright body, blood spurting like a fountain, slowly crumpled forward.

Richard quickly assessed their situation, Walther

217

would have to stay behind, the other three could carry on. He offered Susan a chance to stay behind with Walther.

"Not on your fucking life!..." She asserted, adding, "...You go on, I'll catch up in a minute, I need to sort out Walther's arm." Tsuba, after pressing a small handgun into Richard's palm, was already half way up the path, heading for the back of the house as they had planned.

Richard followed him at a run, branching off to take the front of the house.

*

Inside the house, watching from an upstairs window, Franco had spotted Tsuba and prepared to meet him. The twins, investigating all the commotion, went downstairs to the large hallway; they passed Raven, dashing up the stairs looking for Cairo.

Richard approached the double-front doors at a run, he was surprised when they flew open in front of him, revealing the twins eagerly beckoning him in. He moved forward more warily, meeting them at the steps.

"Richard!" They chorused, smiling. They both took one of his arms and led him into the hallway, Richard's eyes checked every corner for danger, he was afraid of a trap. Still holding his arms the twins spoke in fast cautious whispers,

"Have you come back-"

"To save us-"

"From the evil-"

"That lurks in this house?" They stared at him, waiting for an answer.

"Yes." Was all he could say, he was going to ask where is she? But they spoke first.

218

"It's down there!" The girls pointed solemnly to the floor,

"In that hateful-"

"Laboratory."

Richard automatically assumed that they meant Raven was down in the cellar,

"Show me the way!" He commanded them. Side by side they proudly led him through the kitchen and down a corridor to the top of a dim staircase.

"It's down there!" They shuddered, clung to each other and pointed down the stairs,

"We can't go down there!" He watched them tremble at the thought of it. Still wary of a trap but not knowing what else to do Richard checked his little gun and plunged down into the gloom.

*

Upstairs at the back of the house Franco had confronted Tsuba,

"Turn and leave..." Franco waved his Spanish duelling knife in the direction Tsuba had come, "...Or die."

"Wait, listen to me..." Tsuba didn't want to fight, his vague plan of preventing Richard from attacking Raven already in tatters, "...I'm not here to harm her, I came-" He had to jump backwards as Franco stepped forward with a wide sweep of his knife, "-Listen to me!" But Franco wasn't listening. Tsuba had to defend himself, flashing his Tanto blade rhythmically in front of him. They circled each other, both studying their opponent and the room they were to fight in, looking for a weakness or for a way to take the advantage. Tsuba was younger and faster, Franco was old and wily, a veteran of many such contests.

219

Susan arrived at the front of the house finding the doors wide open, she had seen movement at an upstairs window and assumed that Richard was up there. Waving the big gun in front of her she crossed the wide hallway and cautiously mounted the staircase, taking one step at a time and constantly looking to the top and bottom until she reached the top. On the first floor landing all the bedroom doors were closed except one.

Raven waited inside, seated at her dressing table at the far side of the room with a silver Derringer pistol trained at the door. She could just see through the tiny crack in the door jamb.

Susan could feel her heart beating fast, her breathing quick and shallow, she knew that if someone was in that room they would have heard her approach, taking the initiative she kicked open the door and ran in, firing off a round as she rushed inside.

Raven kept her cool, aimed and fired at the moving target, the small calibre bullet gouging a small but acutely painful chunk out of Susan's lower arm. With a squeal she flashed across the room taking refuge behind the thick wooden headboard and firing off another round in Raven's direction, shattering bottles on the dresser beside her. Involuntarily, Raven fired off her second round that buried itself harmlessly in the headboard, Susan jumped up and quickly took aim before she fired again. The heavy gun blasted a bullet that missed Raven's face by a fraction of an inch, smashing the mirror behind her.

Raven sat motionless, an enigmatic smile on her face, while Susan stood still, watching her, the big gun trained on her. Raven let out a small sigh before uttering,

"Oh why did I choose a gun that only holds two bullets?" She shook her head and smiled, dropping the Derringer to the floor. Susan shouted,

"This is for my mother you fucking whore!" And squeezed the trigger for the fourth and final time.

*

Downstairs, Tsuba and Franco, both bloodied, fought on. Tsuba had drawn first blood with a wide sweeping slash that tore a thin line through Franco's chest, he had replied instantly by moving inside with a lightning fast jab, the fight would have ended there and then had it not been for Tsuba's speed and agility.

*

Richard crashed through the heavy Laboratory door into a hell more vile than even the worst of his nightmares. Nothing could have prepared him for the horror of that ghastly chamber.

The air was fetid with the terrible stench of gore.

Then he saw:

The tilted operating table,

Rita's strapped down body slumped forward in death,

The pool of blood and hair at her feet,

The top of her head missing.

Then he saw:

Sir Clive, his white surgeons gown soaked through with blood,

a scalpel in his left hand and a long-handled spoon

in his right.

The surgeon from hell was chewing something.

A frown of annoyance creased Sir Clive's forehead as he saw Richard, his mouth moved and shouted indignantly,

"You man! What the devil are you doing in here? Get out! Can't you see I'm working!" Sir Clive's outraged manner changed abruptly when he realised that it probably wasn't a good idea if he allowed Richard to leave. Richard was backing up, pale and trembling, he had expected to confront Raven, not this horror.

Sir Clive moved towards him with unmistakable menace,

"No you don't! Stop right there! Come here! You can't leave now..." Sir Clive lumbered forward, scalpel in hand, a dribble of blood dripping from the corner of his mouth. Richard had almost backed up to the door when the mad surgeon leapt at him, knocking him over backwards.

Sir Clive landed on top of Richard pinning him down and stabbing at his face, "...I'm glad you dropped in after all, I have an interesting experiment in mind!"

Shock and fear had made Richard's movements sluggish, it was Tsuba's training that came to his rescue. With a powerful twist he rolled Sir Clive off, punching him in the face at the same time. He rose to his feet breathing hard and staggered backwards towards the door. Sir Clive, making a last desperate attempt, leapt again at Richard embedding the scalpel high in his chest.

Recoiling in pain, Richard violently shoved the older man backwards causing him to fall on his backside. With a groan Richard stumbled through the doorway and slammed it shut. He rammed home the bolts and sagged with his back to the door.

He was trembling uncontrollably and close to fainting when the twins appeared out of the gloom, they ran to his side, helping him to stand,

"Oh Emm, look!" Philippa pointed in distress at the scalpel sticking out of Richard's chest,

"It's a good job we decided to, be brave-" They rushed to him,

"Hold him tightly!" Emm quickly but carefully extracted the blade, the red patch on Richards shirt instantly spreading much further. Richard groaned in pain and cleared his throat before demanding,

"Get me some nails, and a hammer!..." He motioned towards the heavy door, "...Nobody's ever going in there again!..." The twins gaped at him, doing nothing, he waved them away impatiently, "...Go on! Hurry!" He yelled at them as a muffled thumping began on the other side of the door. The girls turned as one and vaulted up the stairs.

*

Cairo appeared in her mother's bedroom doorway in time to see her drop the Derringer to the floor, she saw Susan begin to squeeze her trigger,

"No, no, No! Don't take my mother!" She screamed and ran across the room in front of Raven.

The sudden movement took Susan by surprise; she turned ever so slightly and pulled her shot. The bullet ploughed a thin furrow across Raven's scalp grazing her skull. Cairo turned on Susan, blazing furiously she grabbed a heavy unbroken perfume bottle from the dresser and hurled it at her. It struck Susan on the temple instantly knocking her senseless and raising a lump, she slumped in the corner hidden by the bed.

"Mother? Mother? Are you all right?" Cairo was dreadfully upset and stood before Raven wringing her hands, tears poised in each eye.

Raven groaned and felt her scalp, her fingertips turned red and a thin trickle of blood ran down her face, she shrugged,

"Yes, I think so." She replied sounding slightly dazed. Cairo grabbed her hand,

"We must go! There are men all over the house!" Cairo took her mother's hands and urged her to her feet, but then Raven shook her hands free, her voice loaded with menace,

"Yes, we must leave. But I just want to finish something off first!" She picked up a broken bottle and moved towards Susan.

"No mother! We haven't the time! We must go now!" Cairo pulled Raven by the arm out of the room, she was still too stunned to resist and allowed herself to be led, still clutching the broken bottle, along the corridor to the top of the main staircase.

*

Both men had now been cut twice, Franco on his chest and upper arm, Tsuba on his side and left cheek. They were an equal match and they both knew it. It was Franco's street craft that eventually gave him the upper hand.

Feigning tiredness, he tricked Tsuba into coming too close, allowing him an easy straightforward jab into the chest. But Tsuba's reflexes were phenomenally quick, he managed to evade the deadly strike by a hairs breadth, nevertheless the trick was complete because Franco knew which way Tsuba would turn to evade the strike, he was

224

ready for him as he turned and floored him with a left hook. He was on top of him in a second, his dagger a fraction of an inch from Tsuba's throat when fate intervened. Franco saw movement in the corner of his eye, he paused for an instant as he saw Cairo dragging a bloody-faced Raven passed the open door.

An instant was plenty of time for Tsuba to wriggle his hand free and to twist his Tanto blade into Franco's exposed side, and then he too turned his eyes to the doorway. But it wasn't Raven's face that froze him, it was the black-haired girl beside her that took his breath. The likeness of his own mother in those deep dark eyes.

Franco had lost the fight, he knew he had only a few seconds of life left, he was still on top of Tsuba and could easily finish him off before he died, he waited, staring at Raven in the doorway.

Her face was tragic, she sensed Franco was about to die. And the man he held a knife to the throat of was- *"It can't be."* She thought, *"Tsuba? How~"*

"Come on mother, come on!" Cairo's voice urged as she pulled on Raven's arm. Franco pressed the edge of his blade tight on Tsuba's throat before calling hoarsely to Raven,

"Mistress! Run! Go! Please go!" For a second their eyes locked in understanding, and then she was gone.

Franco lowered his gaze to Tsuba, still held fast beneath him,

"Your life is in my hands..." He rasped out the words, blood rising into his mouth, "...Shall I take it from you?..." Tsuba tried to press himself through the floor as Franco's knife pressed tighter and tighter on his throat, his voice was thick, "...In return for your life I want you to spare my mistress! Let her escape! Do you swear?..." Franco's voice

225

demanded, but his eyes begged. Tsuba nodded, "...Do you swear it?!..." Franco coughed blood, speckling Tsuba's face, "...Swear it damn you!"

"I swear it." Tsuba's words came out in a whisper but they were enough, Franco was satisfied that he had done enough to save his mistress, even at the moment of his own death he cared more for her than himself.

Franco heaved himself off Tsuba, rolled on to his back, and died.

Tsuba, drenched in Franco's blood, hauled himself to his feet and looked down at Franco with profound respect. He bowed slightly as if to an honourable opponent,

"I had no need to swear..." He shook his head in gentle sadness, "...As I tried to tell you, I came not to harm her." He delayed no longer and ran quickly out of the room. He made his way to the front of the house in time to see Raven and Cairo tearing across the gravel in the white convertible, they had escaped. Tsuba raised a hand in salute as the car roared away, his heart relieved, his mind pleased that he would not have to confront Richard.

*

The twins returned to the cellar, one carrying a hammer, the other a bag of nails, they found Richard crouched on the floor with his back to the laboratory door. He looked pale, made worse by that sick light, and his chest was dark red with blood. They heard the muffled thumping from inside the laboratory and shuddered. Richard clambered painfully to his feet, taking the hammer from Emm,

"Pass me a nail." His voice was hoarse and cracking. Pip handed him a four inch nail, with trembling fingers he

226

held it in position and quickly banged it home.

"No one..." He bashed in the first nail,

"...Ever..." He banged in another,

"...Goes in there again!" And another. He kept on nailing the door shut until he was too weak to hold up the hammer, finally falling to his knees with his face pressed against the rough wood.

Tenderly, the twins helped him up and part-carried him to the bottom of the stairs.

"No, stop..." He gasped, "...Wait a minute." Richard shook himself free and stumbled across to an old painted wooden dresser that have been abandoned down there years before.

"Help me shift this!..." He crouched down at one end trying to drag it, "...You two get that end!" Between them they managed to drag the heavy old piece in front of the laboratory door, completely obscuring it. The twins, who had been reverentially quiet up till then, finally found their voice,

"Richard, you must stop now, you're badly hurt..." They each took an arm, "...Come with us upstairs now. We must tend to your wounds. We're getting quite good at sewing."

Richard nodded, feeling deathly tired.

*

Susan 'came to' only seconds after being knocked out but it was more than a minute before she could shake off the dizziness and nausea that followed. She grabbed her gun as she rose unsteadily to her feet. The house had become as quiet as the grave as she staggered onto the landing at the top of the main staircase. Uncertain about

227

what to do next, she decided to go downstairs and look for Richard, gripping the handrail tightly she crept downstairs in silence. Reaching the hallway she saw Tsuba standing motionless in the open front doorway. She walked swiftly over to him hearing a car speed away across the gravel,

"Has she got away?" She asked him, peering outside over his shoulder. Tsuba nodded grimly, staring after the car, trance-like again. Susan pulled him around to face her,

"Have you seen Richard?" She demanded impatiently, shaking him until he was back to normal, his eyes bright and sharp.

"I have not seen him..." He replied, adding, "...But I do not believe he is on this floor." They heard distant hammering.

"The cellar!?" They ran into the kitchen, guessing that it might lead downstairs, inside, cowering but still managing to look defiant, Anjelica and Fidelma clutched kitchen knives, their backs to the wall. It was Fidelma who spoke out for them, her Irish accent even more pronounced than usual,

"Why don't youse just go away and leave us be? We've done you no harm, be off with you!" Susan raised her gun, Tsuba raised his hand.

"No Susan. These people are not our enemy." He spoke more to them than to Susan.

There was a pause while Tsuba searched the eyes of the two women, he spoke softly,

"We mean you no harm." He said,

"Put down your knives and please, tell us where is the cellar?" The two women looked quickly at each other and nodded,

"It's t'rough there!" Fidelma pointed with her knife before placing it on the work surface beside her. Anjelica followed suit,

"I need a drink." She mumbled.

Susan dashed through the door into the corridor that led to the steps down; the hammering had stopped and had been replaced by a loud scraping noise. She hesitated at the top of the gloomy steps, Tsuba beside her.

"Someone's coming up." He whispered. Susan stepped back a pace and raised her gun.

Three figures came into view, a pale and bloodstained Richard helped on either side by two identical looking girls.

"Richard!" Susan gasped out his name, dashing forward to help him. The twins were affronted,

"It's quite all right!-" Emm said frostily.

"We've got him!" Added Pip. They held on to him, steering him on to a kitchen chair. Susan bit her tongue and watched as they peeled off his shirt to examine his wound.

"Not that bad after all-" Emm reported. Pip nodded in agreement,

"A little deeper than last time..." Pip noted, comparing the size of the hole to the scar left after they stitched him up before, "...But we'll soon have you patched up and as good as new again."

*

Cairo saw two figures emerge from the trees as the car sped down the long drive away from the house. She instantly recognised the huge shape of Mr Underhill, the lifeless body of Kelvin Bright slung over his shoulder like a cricket jersey, and a plastic shopping bag containing a heavy-looking round thing in his other hand. She turned, knees on the car seat and waved to him, shouting,

229

"Sorry I didn't have time to say goodbye!" He smiled at her and nodded. The other figure was a man equally as tall as Mr Underhill but only half his stature; he walked beside him holding his left shoulder as if it hurt.

"Von Vohberg." Raven hissed his name. Cairo turned to her mother, smiling,

"Is he a friend of yours mother? He looks like a proper gentleman." Cairo asked as the sped along the gravel.

"No, he's no friend. I knew his father."

"Oh..." Cairo turned back to her mother, "...Are you sure you're okay? After all, you were shot in the head."

"I'm fine..." Raven grinned, "...I've got a very hard head, and it was only a graze." Cairo smiled and looked at the road ahead,

"Where are we going to go?"

"Abroad. Away from this dull, grubby island."

"Where though? Hollywood?" Raven couldn't hold in a snort of laughter,

"Hollywood! Oh daughter you are so-" She stopped herself. Cairo smiled, so happy she had been called 'daughter'. Raven smiled back and put out a hand to stroke her cheek.

"We're going to France. Paris in fact, but first we have to drive to Dover where we can catch a ferry." Cairo turned away, her imagination racing, her voice a whisper,

"Doh-ver to catch a fairy."

*

In the kitchen the twins had finished dressing Richard's wound and he had begun to recover from the shock of the cellar. There was a growing tension between

230

Susan and the twins, with an inner groan he introduced them to each other,

"I'd like you to meet my wife, Susan." The twins jumped as if they'd been bitten,

"WIFE!" The girls exclaimed, their faces horror-struck. They turned and glared at her, their faces full of venom. Then continued, voices incredulous,

"You're-"

"Married-?!"

"To each other?!" There was a heavy silence punctured eventually by the sound of a cork being popped.

"I really need a drink..." Anjelica poured herself a full glass of cool white wine, "...Anybody care to join me?" There were no takers. The twins, in their uncanny way, looked at each other, then fixed their faces in an identical vacant expression. They took a step forward towards Susan, everyone's guard went up, and then the twins stopped. and curtsied,

"Very pleased to meet you." They said. Then spun around and left the room chatting to each other,

"I never thought to ask him, did you?"

"No, of course not. It never occurred to me."

"He might have said something though!"

"Yes I quite agree-"

"Leading us on like that-"

"Should be ashamed!"

Richard let out a sigh of relief when they had gone, Susan eyed him suspiciously, her female intuition working at full-steam maximum overdrive. Then they were all startled when the door flew open, Fidelma marching in with a face like thunder,

"Well this is a fine how do you do! All four of youse standing there chewing the fat while poor Mr Franco's left

231

lying there dead as a gutted rabbit in a pool of his own blood! For goodness sake!"

At that moment Mr Underhill appeared in the other doorway, Kelvin's corpse still over his shoulder. Fidelma fair went in to one,

"Holy mother of God! Another one!" She roared. Everyone stared as she continued her rant,

"Well at least **he's** no loss!..." She waved her hand dismissively at Kelvin, "...No use to man-nor-beast, that one! Not like poor Mr Franco, Such a gentleman..." She wrung her hands, "...We shall have to give him a proper decent burial..." She turned and barked at Mr Underhill, "...Outside wit you and yor filthy cargo!..." She was close to spitting, "...I don't want that foul mess in my kitchen..." She put her palms together, "...Oh sacred mother, whatever are we going to do?" She finally ran out of steam and took a swig from the wine bottle. To everyone's surprise, Anjelica stepped up to take control of the situation, with wine glass in hand,

"Mis-ter Underhill!..." She got his attention, "...Take him..." She wrinkled her nose as she pointed at Kelvin, "... Down to the Sty. The pigs can have him like the others. Then come back here with your shovel, Oh, and on the way back, look for a nice spot in the garden to bury poor Mr Franco." She paused to finish off her glass of wine, Mr Underhill nodded gravely and left.

"And as for you lot..." She pointed towards the door, "...You had all better bugger off! We don't want the police around here any more than you do I'm guessing! So now that the Mistress is gone, and Sir Clive's, erm, no longer with us, I'm going to be in charge. After all, I'm the one who signs for all the bloody housekeeping round here."

Upstairs, the twins bumped into Mai, she looked

232

scared and her eyes were puffy from crying. They comforted her as best they could,

"What is it my dear?"

"Man trouble?"

"Come with us..." They each took an arm,

"...We're going to try on some dresses.

"...Black ones obviously."

*

Richard and Susan, Tsuba and Walther fled outside, they were all lost for words. Tsuba, stripped off his blood-soaked shirt and was first to break the uneasy silence,

"I think our little adventure is over, for the time being." Susan looked unhappy,

"Well, maybe as you say, for the time being. But that bitch is still on the loose!..." Susan had a plan of revenge in mind and it didn't necessarily include Tsuba or Walther, "...Okay Richard. Let's go home" She held his arm. Everyone looked a little uncomfortable. So Tsuba sang:

"Fare thee well for I must leave thee

Do not let the parting grieve thee

And remember that the best of friends must part." Then he bounded away at a run towards the trees.

Walther spoke next,

"Yes, I think it is time perhaps to lick our wounds..." He looked apologetic, embarrassed even, "...I should never have..." He felt a huge amount of guilt and shame for allowing Richard and Susan to become involved, "...I will take you on the boat back to London. You need to find again your lives. You know where to find me when, if, you wish to."

They nodded, turned and watched Tsuba until he

233

was out of sight. Richard felt a pang of loss, he had become fond of the infuriating little man, *"It's not like we could have exchanged addresses..."* He thought, wondering where Tsuba would be heading next, *"...There's so much he didn't say, so much more between him and Raven than he didn't reveal"* He turned back to face Susan and Walther. She was gently massaging his painful shoulder,

"We should head back to the boat, you can lie down for a while." She said. Walther nodded and the three of them turned away from the house, each lost in their own thoughts about what they should do next.

"It doesn't end here, I'm pretty sure of that."

"I never should have let them, but if I had been alone~"

"You may have escaped this time, but I am going to get you sooner or later, and I'm going to cut your fucking head off you fucking bitch."

*

Tsuba. Lines of life, pain, drawn down his face, ran away from the house, *"So close."* He thought, and he remembered the years of pursuit, and of hope, and of anger, and of love. Yes he remembered that emotion. That fucking deceitful treacherous blissful status of living that drove men to madness.

It was late afternoon by the time he had found his way back to the bus. Francesca greeted him,

"Got rid o' him at last?" Tsuba nodded, still lost in thought. He was tired and hungry, she had made no fire so he headed off to forage. Dusk had settled by the time he had prepared some food for them both. She ate noisily between swigging down even more grog than usual. Later

234

he helped her on to the bus where she fell to snoring immediately. Tsuba returned to his fire, his only true companion. He foraged for enough wood to last the night and prepared to sleep beneath the stars.

Tsuba looked into the fire and far far away. Thousands of miles and seventeen years into the past,

"You were carrying my child." visions swam in and out of focus, how they had walked out of Cambodia in 1975, defeated but in love. The years on the road, taking what they needed on the way.

War had taught him to kill.

She had taught him to cry.

Tsuba, the bus

Tsuba woke early the next morning to the sound of birdsong, but it wasn't that sound that woke him. It was the absence of another familiar rasping sound that got his attention, Francesca wasn't snoring. He rose in one movement and moved to the curtain that separated them,

"Francesca...?"He called, listening intently, "...Are you..." he pulled the curtain slightly aside, "...Alrig-?" His voice trailed far away, knowing she was dead the instant he saw her ghastly white visage. She lay propped up in bed with a copy of Troilus and Cressida on her lap, her eyes closed and her jaw slack. Tsuba brimmed with compassion, once again deeply saddened by the loss of another life that had been little more than a flicker. He ground his teeth, unable to block the assault of memories from his younger days, the terrible slaughter, and the loss of his wife. Only she hadn't died. She had left him. Left him drained of all emotion but pity.

He could tell that Francesca had not been dead for

235

long but he wasted no time in tending to her body. Bundling her up in a tight roll of bedding he was surprised how light she was. It was still early morning when he started up the bus and headed for Stratford upon Avon.

The house in the Countryside ~ 2000

Trapped in the cellar Sir Clive gingerly dabbed a wet swab to his bruised face,
a manic grin insinuated itself across his face,
"You can't keep me in here..." He yanked open the drawer containing his surgical tools, "...I'm coming for you..." A heavy and glittering blade reflected his manic eye, "...I'm coming to get you..." He started to scrape away at the wall, knowing that beneath the plaster lay the door to a bricked up room, "...And when I get you..." He scraped and chipped, chipped and scraped, "...I'm going to make you scream."

Return to London

The return boat trip to London had been spent mostly in polite silence. Walther wanted them gone from his life, at least for a while. Susan still seethed, her anger undiminished, her desire for revenge becoming an imperative. And Richard wanted his life back. His business, his best friend, and his wife.
Walther retrieved Susan's car from his garage. They all shook hands on the quayside,
"Take care."

The house in the Countryside ~ 2000

Fidelma pushed her head inside the dumb waiter,

"Holy mother o' god, what th' divil is making that infernal noise?" Anjelica stood behind her, head to one side, just able to make out the faint scratching sound,

"Bleeding rats I shouldn't wonder. Throw some poison down..." She offered helpfully, "...That'll sort out any nasty little monsters lurking down there."

End of Volume 1

Tim is from England.

"The best of times are spent in good company"
I read that somewhere

Birth of the Monster

Judaea ~ AD30

For centuries the art of divining the future from the spilled entrails of ritually slaughtered animals held great acceptance. The diviner, or Haruspex, held the respect of the masses and the ear of the emperor. Haruspex Cassius had a reputation for being the bearer of bad tidings,

"Cloud bringer" They whispered as he passed.

In secret he sought the elixir of life, studying outlawed Pagan magic and conducting experiments in his private chambers, accompanied only by his trusted servant and henchman, Charna.

In a candle-lit chamber the ageing seer peered at the entrails spread before him,

"That one from Nazareth, the one they call The Messiah..." Cassius scowled at his henchman, "...I want his balls."

*

Cassius the Cloudbringer had advised Pontius Pilate,

"Jesus of Nazareth is your enemy; if you allow him to live he will lead an army against you." Pilate nodded in understanding,

"Thank you seer."

*

At the Jerusalem slave market Cassius picked

through the girls on offer,

"No no no! She must be virgin! Let me see." Finally he'd chosen the three girls he needed for his latest, greatest experiment. He bustled them home, dreams of fame and immortality crowding his self-obsessed mind.

*

The day of the crucifixion came, Cassius gave instructions to his henchman,

"Do not disappoint me Charna, and make haste your return!"

Charna watched and waited nervously as Jesus' naked body was scourged with the Flagrum; it was in the moments between torments that he made his move. While the mocking soldiers placed a crown of thorns upon his head, Charna slipped forward, slit his scrotum, removed his testes and ran.

"Hey you!" The soldiers yelled as Charna ran, but none followed him.

An order rang out,

"Get a cloth for his loins..." The centurion scowled, "...There's those in the crowd who will make trouble if they see this."

Charna fled like the wind, heading back to his master with his prize kept warm in goats fur.

Haruspex Cassius was waiting for him,

"Hurry my friend, quickly!" He rushed him through the villa to its inner sanctum,

"Now leave us, return only at dawn!" He slammed the chamber door shut and turned to his drugged-sleeping maidens, his voice high with expectation,

"The fruit you shall bear will bring me great fame

242

and eternal life."

*

But it was not to be so for Cassius.

Two of the girls failed to carry their child full-term. Their reward was to be thrown into the street. The third, Sylvia, gave birth to boy and girl twins. But Cassius was unable to complete his intentions toward the babies because Charna, oft found drunk in the taverns, had boasted of his masters' witchcraft. Cassius was arrested and put to death while Sylvia and her green-eyed babies were taken as slaves by a cousin of the emperor.

The twins, Colum and Raven, grew up in servitude. The boy child was pretty and artistic, the girl with black hair and bright green eyes, was angry and violent, often fighting and always in trouble. Eventually they gave up with her and sent her away to train with the women gladiators.

The boy fared badly in the end, victim to the mad emperor's lust, he died raped and strangled. When the girl found out her brother's fate she shed no tears in public, but made a quiet vow to avenge him some day.

So she devoted herself to the arena and despite her youth became a respected and feared young gladiatrix. The crowds loved her ferocious displays and child-like athleticism, naming her Gladius Angelus and chanting her to victory.

Years went by and despite many wounds, sometimes grievous, she fought on, but eventually rumours started,

"She never gets any older..." Suspicions grew, "...It must be some kind of magic..." People became afraid, "...She must be possessed, a witch!"

And so she travelled, throughout the Roman empire, wherever there was an arena, Gladius Angelus would fight, and scream her own personal battle-cry,

"Angelus Mortem!"

Extracts from Raven - 2

On the plane of the Once-People

Boss Bellini's soul had survived the flames. In fact, it had been *released* by the flames. But it was caged, held in the gaol of the Cinderfolk, a chained up demon soul bellowing for all eternity, on the edge of life, not quite dead. Unless it could find a host. And there are very, very few ways for a lost soul to re-enter life. Someone, someone living, would have to leave the door open for them. Someone with a hole in their life. Someone filled with guilt and can't find a way to punish themselves, perhaps?

Then, somebody could become possessed by a demon.

Susan's bedsit, the mining town

Susan woke with unsettling recollections about the night before, *"Fucking hell did I really-"* she banished the images from her mind and opened a beer. Her mind was broken, shattered. Her recent stress, terrors and ordeals had each taken their toll. And together they had beaten her, she could take no more. She had neither religion nor family to turn to, and she had forsaken her man. She knew she was lost,

"I deserve every fucking thing I get." She brought back into her mind what she could remember of the previous night, *"...They fucking gang-banged me..."* poured beer down her throat, *"...and I yelled out for more..."* she pictured the scar on her cheek, a living brand, *"...It's true, I am a fucking slut."* She rolled over and closed her eyes, swabbing angry tears with her pillow.

Boss Bellini heard her, felt her river of anguish and smiled.

Raven, Riverside ~ Calcutta

She had struck the deal, Hassan Safar would set her up in an apartment, furnished to her own specification, and she would whore for him. He had one major proviso,

"If you don't earn enough **I will have your face!**..." he meant it literally, Raven gasped when he opened a large Rosewood cupboard door, "...See!..." Inside on glass shelves were the skins of several people's faces neatly stretched over mannequin heads, "...You will wish you were made dead!"

Raven recovered her poise,

"Boys..." she smiled as if she hadn't a care, "...always collecting things." Inside she was seething, one part of her wondering if she should use the knife concealed in her hair to murder Hassan while he was off guard, but her sensible side won over, she had a longer~term plan, she would whore for him for as long as it was necessary. Then they would see who would lose face.

Their business was concluded for now, Hassan dismissed her with a wave,

"My men will take you back."

"The front door this time?"

"Don't be ridiculous. How would it look if a whore like you was seen leaving my building, don't be so stupid..." he dismissed her with more vigorous waving, "...And don't ever try to contact me, I will get word to you via my men. And do not ever come to my building, understand!?"

Raven bit her tongue, she followed the guard along

246

the secret back-door route to their car, nothing was said until they were driving, she spoke to the driver,

"Drop me off at my hotel, it's The Broadway."

"I know."

Raven realised she had gotten into some pretty bad shit, and decided to take the rest of the night off, *"No whoring tonight."* She was buzzing inside, Hassan had started a deep longing for satisfaction within her, she had a drink at the hotel bar and then went out for a walk.

She was sated and bloody by the time she returned to her room a little before dawn.

Richard, the Train

Richard played dead as the rebels made their way through the carriage, one carried a sack that was already half full,

"Hand over your money, your phones, jewellery, everything!" A shot rang out, a man's brains flew out of the window, an indiscriminate killing done for effect,

"Everything! We take everything!"

The priest pointed to Coca and raised his voice,

"Murderer!..." and raised his bible, "...Go join your fellow murderers!..." He had the attention of the rebels, Coca raised his bloody knife and saluted them,

"Viva the revolution! Death to the white man!"

The rebels eyed Richard's 'corpse', Coca distracted them by waving some money and his own watch,

"I have his things, see!" he made a show of dropping them in the rebel's sack. The priest intoned a warning from God,

"Those who live by the sword-"

Coca rounded on him and pressed the knife to his

247

throat,

"You want to die too, priest? Shall I cut you open like that stinking white guy?" The rebels were fooled, but they didn't like the idea of killing a black priest,

"Leave him!..." they motioned the priest to move away, "...Go sit over there, and keep your mouth shut!"

Cairo, Malta

Cairo was asleep, but she wasn't dreaming. This time she was remembering, reliving the vivid images she'd seen in the old waiter's anger.

The cafe near the square was newly painted, Cairo walked inside, invisible to the old waiter, Giovanni, now a younger man, and his wife Elena. They lived in a tiny apartment above the cafe, worked long hours together, ate and made love.

Elena died giving birth to a daughter, Kristina.

The cafe was popular, Kristina grew up going to school and helping her father, at first in the kitchen, and when she was old enough she waitressed.

Sometimes she would go out with her school friends, to the beach, or a party. That's where she met Mikele, stormy-eyed and handsome, charming and violent.

At night she would argue with her father,

"If you forbid me to see him it will only make things worse, I will see him behind your back!"

She loved Mikele, there was only Mikele.

*

248